A holiday gift for readers of
Harlequin American Romance

Two heartwarming Christmas novellas
from two of your favorite authors

Christmas Baby Blessings by Tina Leonard
The Christmas Rescue by Rebecca Winters

ABOUT THE AUTHORS

Tina Leonard is a *USA TODAY* bestselling author of more than forty projects, including a popular thirteen-book miniseries for Harlequin American Romance. Her books have made the Waldenbooks, Ingram and Nielsen BookScan bestseller lists. Tina feels she has been blessed with a fertile imagination and quick typing skills, excellent editors and a family who loves her career. Born on a military base, she lived in many states before eventually marrying the boy who did her crayon printing for her in the first grade. Tina believes happy endings are a wonderful part of a good life. You can visit her at www.tinaleonard.com.

Rebecca Winters, whose family of four children has now swelled to include five beautiful grandchildren, lives in Salt Lake City, Utah, in the land of the Rocky Mountains. With canyons and high alpine meadows full of wildflowers, she never runs out of places to explore. They, plus her favorite vacation spots in Europe, often end up as backgrounds for her romance novels, because writing is her passion, along with her family and church. Rebecca loves to hear from readers. If you wish to email her, please visit her website, www.cleanromances.com.

Christmas in Texas

TINA LEONARD

REBECCA WINTERS

Recycling programs for this product may not exist in your area.

ISBN-13: 978-0-373-75431-1

This edition published by arrangement with Harlequin Books S.A.

For questions and comments about the quality of this book,3 please contact us at CustomerService@Harlequin.com.

www.Harlequin.com

Printed in U.S.A.

CONTENTS

Christmas Baby Blessings

Tina Leonard

Dear Reader,

The Christmas season is so magical! Sometimes there's too much hustle and bustle, and it's hard to slow down and think about the real meaning of the season. One of my favorite parts of Christmas is reconnecting with family and friends, whether it's through a Christmas card, a phone call or dropping off a small gift.

Seagal West wants to reconnect with his family, too—specifically his wife! He dearly loves his soon-to-be ex, and once he discovers Capri is expecting their children, Seagal is determined to ring in the holiday with her. Surely there's one more Christmas miracle for them and their new babies?

Capri Snow is resigned to the divorce—she doesn't want him to come back to her just because of the children. Somehow Seagal found out about her pregnancy, and has moved back into their house as her bodyguard. But the only thing she needs protecting from is her own heart!

I hope you enjoy Capri and Seagal's story. There's nothing like Christmas to bring people together, and in Bridesmaids Creek, they're used to matchmaking to help a miracle along. It's my cherished hope that there are many happy memories and a little Christmas magic, too, this holiday season for you!

Best always,

Tina

For anyone who has ever dreamed of the magic of Christmas.

Chapter One

Capri Snow's first thought was that the Santa who sat so alertly beneath the white gingerbread archway of Bridesmaids Creek's Christmastown looked a bit… off. He was tall for a Santa, broad-shouldered, and his tummy had shifted, as if he wasn't comfortable and had tried to move the proverbial bowl full of jelly away from him. If that wasn't odd enough, he was staring at her seven-months pregnant belly as if he were envious of her roundness.

"Come on," her best friend, Kelly Coakley, said, dragging her. "You promised to have a picture taken with Santa for the *Bridesmaids Creek Courier.*"

Yes, she had, so she let Kelly push her onto Santa's lap. There were plenty of things one did on the committee of Bridesmaids Creek's popular Christmastown, and posing for a holiday photo op wasn't a horrible thing. It was just that one of Santa's white eyebrows had come partially unglued, showing his real eyebrows to be jet black, which Capri found a bit unnerving. He pulled her closer, and Capri examined his bearded face. His electric-blue eyes gazed at her intently—and she registered that Santa had much firmer thighs than she would have thought for an elderly manager of holiday elves.

In Bridesmaids Creek, anybody could get roped into

holiday duty. This Santa was probably a hapless dad who'd been talked into the Christmas shenanigans by the authoritative Mrs. Mathilda Penny. "I'm sure Santa has better things to do than pose for the *Courier,* Kelly," Capri said, trying to encourage her friend to hurry it up a bit. Truthfully, she felt very shy about her weight (okay, she hadn't put on that much baby weight, but she felt misshapen and awkward), and something told her it was time to leave Father Christmas's well-muscled lap.

"He doesn't mind, do you?" Kelly beamed. "I bet Santa likes having his picture taken." She clicked a few more photos, enough, Capri thought, for a full spread in a national magazine.

"That's got to be plenty," Capri said, trying to get up from the man's warm lap. She couldn't quite make it to her feet, and Santa gallantly gave her a little push from behind. "Thank you," she said, determined to be polite, though she was well aware he wouldn't have had to give a starter push to a more svelte female.

He blinked at her over the festive snowy beard but didn't reply. Capri decided they'd taken up enough of his time. "Thank you for participating in Christmas-town. We really appreciate it."

"There. That wasn't so bad, was it?" Kelly asked as they stepped away.

Capri glanced back at Santa, whose gaze remained fixed on her as he sat, completely unmoving, on his white Christmastown throne. "That is no harmless elderly Santa."

"I know." Kelly giggled. "He's an undercover cop."

"Kelly!" Capri gasped, astonished. "I know security is tight this year, but I don't think Mrs. Penny would hire an undercover cop to listen to the children's wish lists."

"That's exactly what she did," Kelly said, inspecting her camera with some approbation. "That's Mrs. Penny's nephew. She said that with all the weird stuff going on in Bridesmaids Creek in the past year, she wasn't taking any chances on the safety of the kids. Mrs. Penny loves a good whodunit more than anyone, but I can't disagree with her desire to keep this event safe."

Capri took a fast peek at Santa. His gaze was no longer on her, but trained on some men near the ice sculptures that would greet visitors when the event opened in two hours. The twinkling lights would be on, and Christmastown would be in full swing, overrun by eager tots desiring a turn at Santa's ear.

"Rats," Kelly said. "Sorry, Santa. You'll have to put up with Capri for a couple more seconds. I didn't have the camera set properly." She gave Capri a gentle shove back toward Santa, and it seemed to Capri that Santa reached out for her a bit more enthusiastically than he should have.

Trust Mrs. Penny's nephew to be a diligent St. Nick. Capri once again pasted a smile on her face as Kelly struggled with her camera. Santa seemed happy to have her back on his lap, though he kept his hands off her, which Capri appreciated. The last cop she'd known—her almost-ex-husband—had *never* been able to keep his hands off her.

It was something she badly missed about Seagal.

"Okay, I fixed it," Kelly said. "Smile!"

Capri smiled—then yelped with surprise as Santa shoved her out of his lap, chivalrously making certain she didn't hit the floor. He sprinted toward the ice sculptures and the exit, clearly in excellent physical shape.

Kelly's mouth dropped open. She lowered the camera for a moment, hastily bringing it back up to her eyes to capture the excitement. Santa leaped onto a snow mound complete with festive village snowmen, rolled to the ground and, just as four uniformed police officers converged on the scene, Santa disappeared under a virtual dogpile of bodies.

"I knew he was trouble!" Capri dusted the fake snow from her designer pregnancy jeans and red fuzzy sweater. "Although I'm surprised Mrs. Penny's nephew would be knee-deep in some kind of issue with the law."

"Let's go see what's happening." Kelly pulled Capri with her.

"What happened is that Mrs. Penny's nephew is a bad cop. I'm going to talk to Mrs. Penny and tell her that next year I want her to double-check all the Santas and workers' records for possible felons. And fake cops."

"I don't know," Kelly said. "Looks like he's leading someone off in handcuffs."

Capri watched as Santa and the police escorted what looked to be a very unsavory individual toward a squad car. The police high-fived Santa, and male laughter floated over to her and Kelly.

"At long last Mrs. Penny has a whodunit happen right here in Bridesmaids Creek," Capri said with some disgust. "I'm going home."

"Aren't you going over there to find out what that was about? You're one of the co-chairs of the festival!"

"Mrs. Penny will do the honors more effectively than I ever could. Besides, I've had quite enough of Christmastown for one year, thanks." To be honest, she had a bit of a tummy ache, probably from all the excitement. If she mentioned that to Kelly, her friend would make a federal case of it and send up the alarm that the newest resident of Bridesmaids Creek was about to make its appearance just in time for Christmas. "See you later. Remember, early cleanup tomorrow morning at 8:00 a.m."

"Scrooge!" Kelly accused, but Capri kept walking toward her car. Her stomach was somersaulting like mad. She figured they'd had enough excitement for one night. She got into her small car and drove away.

The police had expected something to happen tonight or else there wouldn't have been an undercover cop dressed as Santa. But they hadn't bothered to tell her, one of the event's organizers.

Something was not good in Christmastown.

TWO HOURS LATER Capri was in her worn flannel pajamas—red and decorated with yellow smiley faces wearing Santa caps—and in no mood to do anything but sit in front of her fireplace and read the cozy mystery Mrs. Penny had lent her when her doorbell rang. Most likely it was her mother, who by now had every bit of news about Christmastown's big night.

"Who is it?"

"Santa!"

The hunky Santa with the bedroom eyes? "Go away," she said, her pride still slightly damaged that he'd shoved her out of his lap so dismissively. "If you're here to discuss future Christmastown employment, you'll have to make an appointment with the event organizer, Mrs. Penny. She hired you."

"Is that any way to talk to one of history's most revered figures? I've heard good Santas are hard to find. And the kids love me."

"Revered indeed." Mrs. Penny lived in the gingerbread-styled house next door and at this hour would have her nose pressed to the glass wondering why a car was parked in front of her neighbor's house. Capri was twenty-seven, but that didn't mean that every single thing she did wasn't dutifully reported to her mother and anyone else with the slightest bit of hearing left.

His voice was familiar; he sounded astonishingly like her almost-ex, Seagal West. But that was impossible. Seagal was with the Texas Rangers, and she wasn't sure exactly where he was working these days. Besides which, Seagal wore Stetsons—she'd bet her last cup of Christmas cheer he wouldn't be caught dead in a festive red Santa cap.

Complete coincidence.

"Go away before you wake my neighbor!" Capri said, though she was dying to know what had happened tonight. Something told her that if she opened the door, she'd be face-to-face with more than a handsome cop. Sexy Santas were not on her Christmas list.

"I've been assigned to you. So open up, doll, before we scandalize the entire neighborhood, and not just the mystery-scribbling Mrs. Penny."

Assigned to her? Capri jerked open the door. He was dressed in regular street wear: casual jeans, loose shirt not tucked in, boots. Standard Stetson, for him.

It *was* the Bridesmaids Creek Santa.

And he was killer handsome, just as he'd always been.

Unfortunately, Santa was also her almost-ex-husband, the only man guaranteed to break her heart. "What do you mean, assigned to me?" Capri demanded. "What is going on, Seagal?"

"Can I come in?"

"Absolutely not." She raised her chin and closed the door an inch. "Say what you have to say right there."

He shrugged, and Capri could tell he was amused by her demand. "Suit yourself. But Mrs. Penny just raised her window about three inches so she can hear us. If you want your business broadcast in Bridesmaids Creek, and rumors of us getting back together—"

"Make it snappy," she said, pulling him inside.

He smiled. "Hello, beautiful."

"Keep it professional, if you're here in a professional capacity, Seagal," she said, realizing she sounded as prickly as a spiny cactus. "Long time, no see."

He glanced at her stomach, and she realized Seagal felt awkward. As if he wasn't certain whose baby she carried.

"Yes, Seagal," she said with a sigh, "we are having a baby."

His whole demeanor changed.

He looked absolutely thrilled.

"That's great!" He followed her as she walked into the formal living room of the house they'd once shared. "Why didn't you tell me?"

"Because you left," she said simply. "You said you needed time to figure things out."

He looked dumbstruck. "I don't need to figure anything out. You were the one who said you had doubts."

This was true. She had said that. The long nights when he was away, the stress of her taking over her grandmother's flower shop, had put a strain on their marriage. She'd been hurt when Seagal left—and scared that if he found out about the pregnancy, he still wouldn't want their marriage. Or worse, he'd find out about the pregnancy and feel as if he had to come back to her out of a sense of misplaced responsibility.

The problem was, she'd always been in love with Seagal, and she knew very well he'd married her because he'd been on the rebound. That fact alone had made her very uncomfortable over the two years they'd been married.

"Capri," he said, "when were you going to tell me about the baby?"

When? When indeed. She hadn't wanted him to come back only to resent her—and he would have. At least, she thought he would have. "I would have let you know before the birth."

"Which is tomorrow?" he said, casting a disbelieving glance at her stomach. "When's the due date?"

She glanced toward the calendar hanging on the kitchen wall. "Hopefully, Valentine's Day." She took a deep breath. "But I've been having little aches and pains I didn't have before. The doctor said it's not anything to be concerned with, but—"

"Good thing I was assigned to you." Seagal sank onto a flowered sofa he'd never been partial to, apparently settling in for the long haul. "I can protect you and be here for the baby's birth."

Capri blinked. "So why do I need someone *assigned* to me? What is going on?"

He looked as if he was considering how much to tell her, and Capri reminded herself that caution had always been one of Seagal's hallmarks. His other sexy hallmarks included jet-black hair and white teeth. A strong, wide chest. He was tall, as tall as her brother, Beau, who was a good six-two. And so handsome she could hardly take her eyes off him, even though they'd barely spoken during the separation.

"Don't water down the story, please," she told Seagal.

"You created the floral displays for Christmastown?" he asked, shifting into cop mode.

"Yes, like I did last year. Everything was almost the

same this year, with a few minor changes, mainly involving the types of flowers that were available."

"This year drugs were concealed in the arrangements. Specifically, pot seeds. They were brought in in the containers you ordered, and then hidden in the bottoms of the vases. It would have been a clever plan if they hadn't been such blabbermouths. And that guy we nabbed was a rush of good information."

She frowned. "Impossible, Seagal. I worked on every one of the displays myself."

He nodded. "I know. That's what Kelly said. They had to have been concealed after you did the designs. Nice pajamas, by the way."

She'd forgotten she was in her happy-face pajamas. And it was late. Mrs. Penny would be having a field day—no doubt her phone line was buzzing. "You have to go, Seagal."

"Actually, I have to stay. Official capacity."

"I don't want the rumor mill starting up, and I'm sure you don't, either."

He made no move to stand. "I could ask for another officer to take over, but frankly, I figured you'd be more comfortable with me in the house than a cop you don't know."

"Not quite," she said, fibbing like mad. No one would believe that the two of them staying under one roof was coincidental or official. That was the problem. "What happened to Mrs. Penny's nephew? Kelly said he was supposed to be the Santa."

"Last-minute change." Seagal looked pleased about that. "Why didn't the proverbial grapevine let me know I was going to be a dad? Even in Dallas, I should have heard about it from my old cop buddies here in town.

My partner usually keeps me informed of the news in Bridesmaids Creek."

She frowned. "Because I didn't tell anyone you were the father. Only Kelly knew."

"Ouch."

Capri sat down, finally deciding Mrs. Penny's curiosity was going to have to wait. "It seemed best, considering our situation."

She didn't think she'd ever seen her husband look more unhappy, except when they'd decided to separate.

"The divorce is final in two weeks," he said quietly. "The day after Christmas. You weren't planning on giving us much of a chance to get back together."

"Because of a pregnancy?" Capri shook her head. "Seagal, if you'd wanted to come home, you would have long ago."

"I can't blame you for feeling that way." He cast a longing eye at her stomach. "You look beautiful, by the way."

Secretly she was flattered, even if she knew Seagal was being kind. "Thank you."

He nodded. "It's true."

She didn't say anything else. Things were too uncomfortable between them as it was.

"What are we having?"

She looked at him, seeing real interest in his eyes. "I don't know. I didn't want to find out," she fibbed.

"I'm going to be there," he said softly.

He leaned back on the sofa, trying to seem casual. The depth of his voice told her that Seagal was anything but casual.

"All right. Just no looking under the sheet or seeing me naked."

He smiled. "Always good to know the ground rules."

Her heart beat a little harder at his smile, but she'd always loved Seagal's smile, and just about everything about him. "Will you be comfortable sleeping on the sofa?"

"Well, I'd be more comfortable in our—"

"You're familiar with the kitchen, I'm sure," she interrupted. "I'm not happy about you being here, but I guess Mrs. Penny will just have to have some gossip with her bagel in the morning."

Shrugging, he scooted down in the sofa and closed his eyes. "Good night."

She studied her almost-ex-husband. "Exactly what is it you're protecting me from?" she asked, thinking she was in far more danger from Seagal.

His eyes remained closed. "The man we arrested today was part of a small-time gang using your shop to transfer drugs. Now he's in jail, but someone else will take his place. Your shop might have proven to be convenient. We want to bust this crowd, but obviously we don't want you caught in the middle, since there may be hometown boys involved."

"I don't know a single person in BC who would dabble in illegal drugs," Capri said. "We have our troublemakers, but no one who would do something like that. If there really are drugs in Bridesmaids Creek, they have to be coming from the outside."

Seagal shrugged. "I can't say any more than I have. But I'm hanging out here with you until the BC guys have everything pinned down."

She didn't want Seagal in close quarters with her. No telling what might happen if they shared a roof.

They'd shared a bed before—that part of their marriage had been wonderful. But a marriage wasn't built solely on sexy fun.

"I can close the store for a few days," Capri said, knowing that wasn't really feasible. She had employees to think of, and arrangements already ordered for holiday parties and even a wedding.

"That would stop the traffickers for a few days, but not the long term. Simpler to just catch them while the situation's hot."

Capri eyed her husband lying on the sofa he'd never been keen on—he'd far preferred the leather sofa in the den—and thought he looked sexier than the last time she'd seen him. He'd shattered her heart when he'd left, and now he was back, wanting to protect her, and see his child born.

The situation was *definitely* hot.

"This is not the way to spend Christmas," she said. "Haven't you heard that holidays are stressful?"

He pushed his Stetson low on his face. "Then don't stress me out, dollface."

Stress *him* out? She was pregnant, someone was using her grandmother's shop for illegal activity and her sexy about-to-be-ex husband wanted to be her bodyguard.

"Merry Stressmas," she said, and went off to bed.

Chapter Two

Seagal let himself out of Capri's house the next morning to check the perimeter of the small, three-bedroom home. The fact that his wife and child might be in danger chilled his blood. He'd nearly had heart failure when he'd heard that the feds were nosing into a drug ring in Bridesmaids Creek—and who should be involved but his darling, everybody's-best-girl, almost-ex-wife.

Imagine his shock when he learned from a very reliable source that his wife was about to make him a dad. Heart failure. Capri had always brought him to his knees, but now...now she staggered him.

She hadn't planned to tell him. He knew Capri better than she realized. Oh, she would have told him after the birth of his bundle of joy, and not one second before.

Because she knew he'd be right back here in Bridesmaids Creek—and she didn't want him back.

Tough. She was going to have him. That baby was going to know its dad—no matter what sexy mama had in mind.

"Hey!"

Seagal glanced up. His fellow officer Jack Martin idled at the curb in one of Bridesmaids Creek's new police cruisers. He strolled over to greet Mrs. Penny's nephew.

"What's up, Jack?"

Jack grinned. "Considering that your car is parked in Capri's driveway, I'm surprised you are."

Seagal ran a hand over his unshaven chin. "Just barely. Did you bring me a latte, or is this a social call?"

His buddy grinned. "Neither. Just wanted to let you know that you were a hit last night. The kids said you were the best Santa ever. You've been voted Santa Most Likely to Repeat next year."

Seagal grunted. "I couldn't get out of that itchy suit fast enough."

"Scrooge." Jack handed him a coffee in a white cardboard cup. "Have a jolt on me. Figured you didn't sleep much."

Seagal sipped the beverage gratefully. "I didn't. As sofas go, it's not made for sleeping. I always despised that flowery thing, and now it's my bed. I think that's called karma. I wanted to get rid of it, and somehow that poufy nightmare outlasted me."

Jack laughed. "Does my aunt always keep an eye on you like this? I'd like to think she's proud of me, but I'm pretty sure she's got her radar trained on you."

Seagal glanced over his shoulder, waving at the pink-roller-wearing Mrs. Penny. She had a white phone tucked firmly up to her ear, chatting away. Mrs. Penny waved back, thrilled to have been noticed. "You know your aunt and her friends run this one-horse town. If it wasn't for her, we'd still be—"

"The creek no one ever heard of." Jack put the cruiser in Drive. "True, but you're definitely in her sights for the next few weeks. Just so you know. I won't be down the street before she calls me wanting to know all."

"I'm good with it. She makes great chocolate chip cookies."

Jack grinned. "I know. By the way, I was told to give you a nudge to snoop around your wife's flower shop."

Seagal's cup didn't quite make it to his mouth. "What am I looking for?"

Jack shrugged. "Anything suspicious. Especially check out the employees, and anyone who seems to hang around a lot. You get the idea."

"Yeah, but—" Seagal considered what Jack was saying. "The drugs could have been moved after Capri put the arrangements out at Christmastown."

"Probably. Just check around."

Jack drove off. Seagal grabbed the newspaper lying on the sidewalk and waved to Mrs. Penny before heading inside the small painted house, ruminating on how he could snoop around Capri's shop without getting her annoyed at him. She'd always been super-independent. And they weren't on the world's best terms.

Now he had to scope out her business *and* her home.

Nothing good could come of this.

"Good morning." He looked at Capri as he walked into the kitchen. She seemed pale, not her usual sparkly self. "You all right?"

Capri picked up her purse. "I had a little stomach upset last night. It kept me up, so I'm going to let Dr. Blankenship check me over."

"I'll drive you," Seagal said quickly.

She looked at him. "Kelly's going to take me, thanks. Don't you have work?"

He did—her. "Nothing I can't handle. Cancel Kelly and let me sub in. A dad should be there if his young son is causing his mother heartburn. And anyway, isn't Kelly part of the Christmastown cleanup team this morning?"

Capri hesitated. He loved how she'd pulled her blond

hair up into a bouncy ponytail to get it out of her face. She no longer wore the skinny jeans and cute cropped sweaters she'd once favored, but she was still all kinds of beautiful as far as he was concerned. Sexier than ever, actually. He felt his own heart get a little burn in it that had nothing to do with anything he'd eaten and everything to do with his wife keeping him at arm's length.

"Yes, she is. So am I, but Dr. Blankenship said I could cross that fun off my list immediately." She looked at Seagal. "I guess you can take me to the doctor. Thank you."

"Great." He grabbed his keys and tried to help her to the front door. Capri waved him off. "Because I was about to play the guilt card on you."

"That would be a new one," Capri said.

He thought she sounded tense and realized she didn't feel well at all. "Hey, you want me to carry you?"

"No," Capri said. "I want you to walk very slowly and don't do anything to get Mrs. Penny in a lather."

"Too late," Seagal said, waving again to Mrs. Penny. It seemed rude not to acknowledge her at her lace-festooned lookout.

"It's going to be all over town that you spent the night," Capri said, not thrilled.

"Yeah, well. Could be worse, right? Could have been her nephew, my buddy Jack."

He helped Capri into the car. She eased in as though she was trying not to disturb fragile packaging. "Are you sure I shouldn't take you straight to the hospital?"

"I'm fine." Capri put a hand on her stomach and looked out the window, deliberately avoiding his gaze. He pulled out of the drive, resisting the urge to mash the pedal to the floor.

"You're almost seven months pregnant," Seagal said. She'd kicked him out—though she claimed he'd left—four months ago. "How did I not notice?"

"Even I didn't know." Capri sighed. "The first trimester was a dream. I didn't realize I was pregnant until the end of the third month. The second trimester was more difficult, at least for me. I didn't start showing for quite a while, I guess because I'm tall." He felt her gaze on him. "I did have a little bit of stomach distress when you were still here, but I assumed it was extreme annoyance. So I ignored it."

He grimaced. "Turned out it was a baby?"

She sighed. "You might as well know. There are two. Not even Kelly knew that."

Seagal slammed the brakes at the stop sign out of pure reflex. "Two what?"

"Babies."

Shock. Brain-hit-with-a-stun-gun shock. "We're having twins?"

"That's right. Drive. I don't want to be late."

Seagal couldn't get any words past his throat. No wonder Capri seemed so big. She *was* big. "When were you going to tell me?"

"When you got over the initial shock of finding out you were going to be a father."

He grunted, his heart racing. Two? There were no multiples in his family, or hers, as he recalled. "How did that happen?"

"You made love to me a lot," Capri said, "and something hit bingo would be my guess."

He *had* made love to her as often as possible. To be honest, making love to Capri was pretty much the best part of his day. He missed it like crazy.

He missed *her* like crazy.

"I should never have left," he said. "You talked me into a separation, but I knew better at the time. I was right. We belong together."

She shrugged. "Not because we're going to be parents, Seagal. Children won't fix what was wrong with our marriage."

He parked in front of the doctor's office. "Sit right there and do not move, Miss Independence. I'm coming around to shoehorn you out. I'm afraid if you move the wrong way, we'll have babies sooner rather than later."

Seagal hurried around to help her out of the car, amazed that his wife actually remained seated, patiently waiting for him. The soft blue dress fell around her tummy, catching his eye. It looked as if a watermelon had taken up residence inside his delicate wife. He eased her from the seat, trying to brace her. "I came back not a moment too soon, I can tell. I'm not leaving your side, Capri."

"Obviously," she said, sounding as though she was gritting her teeth a bit. "You're assigned to me."

"That's right," he said cheerfully, reminded that she couldn't dislodge him even if she wanted to.

"*Assigned* isn't the same thing as marriage," Capri said, walking slowly into the doctor's office. "You can stay with me until the cops figure out that I'm not in any danger. The whole drug thing is purely a coincidence. Then you can go back to wherever you came from."

That didn't sound good. Seagal wisely kept his mouth shut, hovering over his wife as she checked in, then helped her to a chair. He received several smiles from the other women in the waiting room and relaxed a bit. His wife was going to have to get over her idea that their marriage was a foregone failure.

He hadn't come back to fail. When Beau, Capri's beloved "baby" brother, had told him that Capri was having a baby, he'd pulled every department string possible to get himself assigned to the case—and ultimately, to her. Having worked his way up in the Texas Rangers, he was something of a hometown hero. It hadn't been hard to get assigned back to BC.

It was terrifying to think he had only two weeks to win back his wife.

Capri would be mad as a little bee if she knew how determined he'd been to get back into her life. He'd wanted to keep her out of danger the second he heard about the case building in Bridesmaids Creek. But when he'd heard that she was pregnant, Seagal had known he had to move heaven and earth to be with her.

And he wasn't leaving her ever again—not if he could convince his opinionated and cutely stubborn little wife otherwise.

"TOTAL BED REST," Dr. Blankenship said. He gazed sternly at Capri.

The expression on the doctor's face unnerved Seagal. Rarely had he seen the physician look so concerned.

"Bed rest?" Capri said. "I have a lot to do. I'm doing the flowers for a wedding. I'm also scheduled for some Christmas parties—"

"Total bed rest," Dr. Blankenship cut in, shaking his head. "We talked about you needing to be in bed last week, Capri."

"What?" Seagal looked at Capri in disbelief. "What were you thinking?"

"That I had Christmastown to set up, and that Dr. Blankenship is overprotective. I've known him since I was a child. He's always been from the old school of medicine." She tried to lever herself off the table, and both men jumped to assist her.

"No," Dr. Blankenship said. "Capri, these babies are going to come early if you don't stay off your feet. And the longer they stay in you, the better off they will be. Do you want them inside you growing and getting the nourishment they need naturally, or do you want to take precious time from them? They could end up with immature lungs or other complications," he warned, his gray eyes filled with disapproval.

"All right. You're right. Of course you're right. I don't know what I was thinking." Tears jumped into Capri's eyes, stunning Seagal. He'd seen Capri cry once, maybe, in all the years he'd known her. Doc Blankenship handed her a tissue, which she took gratefully, blowing her nose. "I've never been the kind of person to lie around."

"I know." The doctor looked at her with the first bit of a smile he'd worn in the past half hour. "But going ninety to nothing isn't going to benefit you or the babies. You can press Kelly into service for help with the wedding arrangements, can't you?" He regarded Seagal cautiously. "Are you back in town for good now?"

"Yes," Seagal said, stressing the word with a glance at his wife.

Capri looked away, fidgeting with her tissue.

"Then you stay on her," Doc Blankenship said. "It's absolutely critical that Capri remain at home in bed. I should have forced her on this issue last week, but she assured me she was fine."

"I am fine," Capri said. "Or I was until last night."

"Clearly I returned not a moment too soon." Whether she liked it or not, he intended to be a pain-in-the-butt nurse, sticking to her like glue.

He knew Capri would resent his intrusion. Resist his efforts to take care of her. She'd barely accepted his role as bodyguard; bodyguard with a nursing specialty she'd like even less.

But she was still his wife. And he loved her, even if she thought she was over him.

Chapter Three

"Comfy?" Seagal asked Capri after he'd taken her home, given her a scolding in his overbearing I'm-taking-charge-now, I'm-a-cop, this-is-what-I-do-best tone, and then tucked her in her bed.

Their bed.

She glowered at him. "This isn't going to work. I want you to call Kelly and tell her to hire someone to help me. It doesn't need to be all the time, for heaven's sake."

"For when I'm out of the house." Seagal nodded as if her suggestion made sense. "Good idea. I'll call her now."

"No," Capri said, trying not to snap at him. He was just too big, too good-looking, overpowering the small bedroom where they'd spent many happy hours.

"I don't want you here. You're going to drive me insane."

"Well, that is a personal problem, I believe," Seagal said, dragging one of her pretty upholstered chairs into the bedroom. "I would drive you insane no matter what, so I might as well go for broke." He flung himself into the stuffed, sweetly patterned chair that went with the floral sofa that had so offended his masculine sensibilities. "You covered these chairs. They were denim blue. Now they're—"

"Toile," Capri said, knowing he wouldn't know what that meant. "To go with the floral sofa and the delft-blue paint on the walls, the delicate gold-foil mirror over the white fireplace mantel, and the special cushions I had made for the two ladderback chairs. Sort of country-French appeal I call it." She smiled at him. "It's a feminine room. Not a place for hanging deer heads and hunting rifles."

"I know." He grimaced. "And you changed the comforter on the bed. It's *lacy*."

"And white." Capri enjoyed Seagal's perplexed expression. "I gave up the masculine decorating scheme after you left."

He looked at her. "We'll discuss that another time. You just rest right now. You need the rest, and so do my sons. Clearly, you aren't any better at obeying doctor's orders than you are a husband's."

She tossed a pillow at him, catching him in the face. "Don't go all pigheaded to try to get me off the subject. Call Kelly."

"You'll hardly notice I'm here. I'm serving a dual role that none of your girlfriends can fulfill."

"Annoying me and wearing out the new furnishings?" She smiled sweetly. "As I said, this isn't going to work. You're too bossy—"

"And you're stubborn as heck. What woman thinks decorating for Christmastown is more important than her own babies?" Seagal demanded. "You always said that my responsible side weighed your flighty side."

"But I didn't necessarily mean that it was a good thing." Capri thought about it. "To be honest, Dr. Blankenship didn't say I absolutely had to go to bed last week, Seagal. He said it would be best, and that he preferred to err on the side of caution. You know John Blankenship," she said, trying to make him see she wasn't being reckless with her pregnancy. "He advises most of the town to stay away from the Wedding Happy Bakery because he says the magic in their secret batters is guaranteed to clog arteries just from looking at the cookies and cakes. He's a fine doctor, but he's been known to be a bit of an alarmist."

"Maybe. But not where babies are concerned. He's seriously planning to send a nurse out here with a drip if your contractions don't go away." He studied her, not happily. "You're just going to have to accept the fact that I'm here for the long haul, babe."

"I don't think so," Capri said, knowing steam was probably pouring out of her ears. If Seagal thought he was just going to waltz back into her life and start being an overbearing donkey, he could just go bray elsewhere. "Hand me the phone."

He got up, seemed to consider her words, then paced down the hall. "We'll continue this discussion in a moment."

"He acts as if I didn't take care of myself for the past several months." Capri reached for the phone on her bedside table, finally hooking it with the aid of a slipper she pulled off her foot. She dialed Kelly's number.

Kelly's cheerful voice shouted a hello. Capri switched the phone to her other ear, hoping the eardrum wasn't bruised. "I need a favor."

"What?"

"Doc Blankenship's put me on bed rest. As in, don't move a fingernail."

"Oh, man. You are going to lose your mind," Kelly said.

Capri sighed. "I need a personal assistant."

"Isn't Seagal in the house with you? Kind of dishy for a personal assistant. I bet if you put him in an apron—only an apron—he'll be your dream come true."

Capri winced. "I do not want to put Seagal in an apron or anything else."

"Don't share," Kelly said. "I'm too busy trying to have my own sweet dreams about his buddy, Jack. Nothing's happening on that front, but that doesn't mean I don't have my radar trained on him."

"Kelly," Capri said, "if you could be here, Seagal and I wouldn't be alone together. And then sometimes he'd leave, go do some cop stuff."

"Oh." Kelly was silent for a moment. "I'd love to help you out, but I can't. I'd never forgive myself if I messed up this chance for the two of you to work things out. I owe it to my darling godchildren to help you two wonderful, well-intentioned but obstinate friends realize that marriage means two people in the same bed. You are my dearest friend, even if you didn't tell me about the twins," Kelly said.

"I will name a baby after you if you help me."

"You're having boys," Kelly said. "Does Seagal know he's having boys?"

"The name Kelly is appropriate for a boy or a girl," Capri said with some disgust at her friend's lack of loyalty. "No, he doesn't know, and you're not telling him. Besides which, it turned out that the early sonograms were wrong. Baby Snow is having a twin sister."

"Snow?" Kelly didn't say anything for a moment. "Does Seagal know you're using your maiden name?"

"No." They were two weeks from a divorce; she had to be practical.

He was going to hit the roof.

"You're really not focusing on what's important.

What is important is that I'm big as a house, I feel stuffed like a Christmas turkey and I don't want Seagal sitting here looking at me when I could do stand-ins for the blueberry girl in *Willy Wonka.* I'm feeling distinctly unlike my former more slender self," Capri said.

"It's all right," Kelly soothed. "Seagal probably likes a little more woman than less."

Capri sighed. "You are not helping. And you're not going to, are you?"

"Not the way you want me to," Kelly said. "But I'll bring you some carrot cake from the Wedding Happy Bakery," she said, her voice brightening.

"Oh, that's just what I need—mach-five calories. How'd the cleanup go, by the way? Did everything get put away properly for next year? Did—"

"Relax," Kelly said. "Believe it or not, we took care of everything even without your capable guidance and your megaphone. Now rest, my godchildren."

Kelly hung up, and Seagal walked back in the room, slinging himself back into the puffy chair. "Your mother brought you a casserole. My favorite." He looked pleased, not noticing Capri's outrage. "I put it in on the counter. It's all warm, and she brought nice toasty bread because she heard I was staying here with you. I always loved your mom," he said, practically sighing in anticipation of the meal. "She didn't want to come in. But she gave me a very mother-in-lawly hug and said welcome home."

She glared at her almost-ex. "Seagal, you are not staying here."

"It's either me or Jack."

"I'll take Jack," Capri said definitively.

Seagal looked hurt. "You know he gossips. Like a girl. And if he's here, Kelly will be here all the time. I don't know why he doesn't get that she's crazy about him."

"I don't know why men have such thick skulls," Capri said. "They just don't get what females are trying to tell them sometimes."

"Yeah, I know." He sighed. "It's an honest mistake. A disconnect, even. Excuse me."

"Where are you going?"

He didn't answer, strolling down the hall. She heard the front door open, and Seagal's voice cheerily greeting someone. Then the door closed and he made it back to his chair.

"Apple pie," Seagal announced. "Courtesy of Mrs. Blankenship. Guess Doc told his wife you were in need of something sweet."

"Is there a reason the doorbell isn't ringing?" Capri asked.

"I disconnected it," Seagal said, obviously pleased with himself. "You need to rest. I didn't want you waking up when my cop buddies drop by."

This was one of the problems they'd never been able to overcome. "There's that disconnect you were talking about," Capri said. "That man-woman disconnect."

"Well," Seagal said, "it's going to be a long couple of months. You might as well make like a bear and hibernate back here under that lacy comforter." He looked longingly at the bed.

She slid the phone under her pillow so he wouldn't decide to commandeer that, as well. "Go away, Seagal."

A snore caught her attention. Just like the old days, Seagal had dropped off like a tired baby. Even snoring he looked handsome, and she thought about tossing another pillow at him.

She wished he was sleeping in her bed, as he once

had. Most nights they'd barely moved, completely curled in each other's arms.

It could *not* be.

She closed her eyes, relaxing now that Seagal wasn't watching her. As long as he was sleeping, he wasn't in her business.

That was good. It was what she wanted. She didn't want to start feeling close to Seagal again, not now.

She might be in bed on doctor's orders, but she wasn't going to hand her heart to her husband again—even if it was terribly hard not to remember that once upon a time he'd meant everything to her.

"AT LEAST you're not lonely," Kelly said, grinning at Capri as she put a beautiful Christmas-themed bouquet of flowers on the dresser in Capri's room. "If you think about it, matters could be a lot worse. I would love to have a hunky man hanging out in my bedroom."

Capri looked at her highly energetic friend. "I still say you only have to ask Jack and you'd probably get your wish."

Kelly sat down in the chair Seagal had dragged into the room yesterday, making himself at home in her room between visits and calls from his buddies and her friends who continuously dropped off food. He hadn't yet let anybody past the front door.

"I think Jack's got his eyes on someone else."

Capri looked at her friend. Kelly's hair was pulled up on top of her head in a flaming-red knot of bouncy fun. Dangling Christmas ornaments hung from her ears, shiny red-striped balls that screamed festive. Capri did not feel festive. "Jack never dated much. Who do you think it is?"

"I think Daisy Donovan." Kelly's face grew downcast, a counterpoint to the happy ornaments bobbing at her cheeks. "I saw them hanging out at the burger joint last night."

Capri wrinkled her nose. "I don't think Jack would date a woman that Seagal was once very serious about."

"Serious until he fell for you," Kelly reminded her.

Capri always felt pain at the mention of Daisy. "What happened was that they dated for a year. It got too serious, and Daisy decided she wanted to date other people. I jumped on the chance to ask Seagal out." She shrugged. "We went out, and I'm not ashamed to say we had a very good time. I wasn't trying to steal him from Daisy, but I wasn't about to leave him in the pond if she'd decided to cast him back."

"Point being, he fell for you." Kelly grinned. "You're lying in this bed because he's crazy about you."

"That's the thing," Capri said, "I've always felt like I did steal him from Daisy. And I think Seagal secretly was still in love with her, but she kept dating Ryder Holland, and so there I was."

"Yes," Kelly said, "there you were. Warm and willing. Always a smart woman. Valedictorian of our class for a reason."

Capri moved restlessly, pulling her sheets over her huge stomach. The babies kicked and she put a hand on them to try to calm them. They stayed active almost all the time now, trying to claim space, she supposed. "They would have gotten back together if I hadn't jumped on Seagal."

"So?" Kelly laughed. "*If* is the biggest, most dramatic word in the English language. Anytime you hear someone say *if,* hang on. There's a story coming."

"It's true. Not that I feel guilty about it. I just feel that I never had Seagal in the first place."

"Because you didn't date that long before he led you to the altar." Kelly nodded. "Everybody was amazed at how quick Seagal was to jump to say 'I do.'"

"And then he said 'I don't.'" Capri frowned, remembering. "We didn't think things through before we got married."

Kelly leaned back in the toile chair, wagging a finger at Capri. "He's a man of action. You're the thinker in the relationship. You want to plan everything to death. Just for once in your life you let yourself get swept, and now you want to overthink it. You're going to have to accept that Seagal's approach to dating was how you won a very handsome husband. And now you're having his twins. Nothing like sweet babies to make a man love a woman even more."

She wasn't sure love was what guided Seagal. "He's been an absolute general ever since he got back in the house. If he hadn't needed to make a run, you wouldn't even be allowed in here."

"I bribed him." Kelly grinned. "I told him I wanted to spend time with Jack. So here I am."

"Jack isn't here."

"Jack's skulking around somewhere. He's your bodyguard, for the moment." Kelly waved a languid hand. "Lying low, protecting his best friend's girl."

"This is ridiculous. Nothing's going to happen to me!" Capri leaned back against the pillows, annoyed. "I don't appreciate Seagal taking over my life like this. He's going to hear about it, too." If she had to lock him out to convince him that no one was coming in and no one was going out—and that included him—that was what she was going to do. "Go find Jack. Drag him off for some alone time. Get him out of my bushes or out of my driveway. Seduce him, if necessary. Please, for my sake."

Kelly considered this advice. "If I lure Jack away, Seagal will never allow me to be his stand-in to help you. It was everything I could do to convince him that you'd be fine with me sitting with you."

"Help me up. I'll tell Jack there's fresh apple pie in the kitchen. Then the two of you can at least sit in the kitchen and chitchat instead of you wilting at my bedside. How do you expect to lure him away from Daisy if you're not setting your lures out?"

"I don't know," Kelly said, "I'm not much for baiting. Lie down!" She glanced at the door, then got up. "I'll go see if I can find Jack, if you promise not to move. I'll only be gone five minutes."

Capri warily settled back against the pillows. "If you find him, stay gone as long as you want. Nothing can happen to me while I'm lying in bed, for heaven's sake. Don't make me regret trusting you on this mission. I need relief from Seagal in my life."

Kelly shot out of the room to find Jack. Capri grabbed the phone from under her pillow and dialed her husband. "Seagal. It's Capri."

"What's wrong? Is everything all right? I can be home in five minutes—"

She sighed. "I don't want Jack posted as lookout outside and Kelly as sentry at my bedside. I want my house back. Can you understand that?"

"You're on complete bed rest," Seagal said, aggravatingly sure of his stringent application of Dr. Blankenship's orders. "You need help. We all want to help."

"I know," Capri said, "but this is driving me crazy. I just need to spend these last few days thinking about the beautiful children I'm about to have."

Seagal came walking down the hall, holding his cell phone to his ear. When he saw Capri alone in the bedroom, he clicked his phone off, shoving it into his jeans. "Where's Kelly?"

"In the powder room, I think." She didn't worry about the fib; Seagal's face was creased with lines of worry. "You seriously need to relax, Seagal. I took care of myself before you showed up—"

"But I'm here now and will be here until the end." He sank into the chair, looking a bit dazed. "You scared me. I thought you were having more pains."

"That's the problem. You shouldn't be scared. There's nothing to be afraid of." She glared at him. "Where were you just now when I called you?"

Seagal looked sheepish. "Mrs. Penny called me over for a chat. And some cookies."

Capri's lips pursed. "I see. She wanted information about the arrest at Christmastown the other night, or wanted to know why you're suddenly back in the house with me?"

His eyes met hers with wry acknowledgment. "Both. Of course."

"You sold out your conscience for some cookies."

"I sold it for gingerbread men. It was completely worth it, too. They had frosting sweaters with mint buttons baked on them. I'm a weak man when it comes to Mrs. Penny's baking, Capri."

He was the least weak man she'd ever known. In fact, Seagal was the strongest person she'd ever met in her life, other than her mother and father. He sat there in a black long-sleeved shirt, his hair not exactly appearing combed—he'd probably sprinted from next door, a day of stubble on his face.

Darn him. She'd never gotten over him.

"Seagal," Capri said, "I don't want you staying here."

He shook his head. "Don't be mad because I didn't bring you any cookies. Mrs. Penny said she's bringing over a box later. That's why she baked them."

She shook her head, not allowing him to sidetrack her with cookie romance.

"I have to stay here with you," Seagal said. "Those are my children. You're my wife. There's no place on this earth I belong more than right here."

Her heart tugged painfully. "Seagal, if you hadn't found out I was pregnant, you wouldn't be here. You weren't coming back to Bridesmaids Creek. We'd be at the courthouse in two weeks, signing divorce papers."

He shrugged. "I came back to Bridesmaids Creek because I heard you were expecting. I didn't know it was twins, but all the same, I knew you were having a baby. And Beau assured me it was mine."

"What?" Capri yelped, stung by her brother's betrayal.

Seagal ignored her. "I didn't have to come back. To be honest, I asked to be on this case. I didn't know you were going to be assigned round-the-clock protection—"

"Which is dumb," Capri said. "I don't need a bodyguard."

"But I did want to be there when the bust went down," Seagal said, ignoring her. "I just wasn't expecting you to be so far along. Once I saw you, I knew I was the bodyguard my wife required."

"Seagal, I don't need you or anyone. I can take care of myself and these children."

"I know you can," Seagal said, "but you married me for better or worse. You're stuck with me, gorgeous. At least for another few days."

He was so unmovable. Determined. "Stuck is right," she said with a sigh.

Seagal stood. "I wasn't happy you didn't tell me, but then that's when I realized you were still in love with me, and that you'd never gotten over me."

Capri's jaw dropped at Seagal's outrageously high opinion of himself. "How does that even work?"

"Because—" Seagal said, sliding up into bed with her, his boots dangling over the edge of the lacy white comforter "—you were never that good at fibbing, Capri. And you weren't going to tell me, because you knew I'd be here in a heartbeat." He turned to look at her, too close for her comfort. "I knew if I came home, you'd have to look me in the eye and tell me you honestly didn't love me anymore. And you can't do that."

She didn't say anything. Yet she couldn't look away from his deep blue eyes, either.

"Can you say you don't love me anymore, Capri?" Seagal asked, and when she couldn't bring herself to say she didn't, he leaned over and brushed his lips against hers.

Chapter Four

Seagal looked at his annoyed wife, feeling his blood pressure subside. He'd kissed her ever so slightly to comfort her, but now she was even more worked up and looking suspicious of his intentions. Capri really had worried him, and that's when he knew she had a point: he worried about her constantly now.

He'd kissed her to comfort himself.

Feeling her lips against his was something he needed. He did still love her, no matter what doubts she had squirreling around in that cute head of hers.

"Sorry," he said. "Won't happen again."

"It better not," she shot back. "And now, if you don't mind, impertinent sir, could you please remove your boots and self from my bed?"

Seagal got up. "It's this white lacy comforter thing. It's like a man defender. I'm afraid I'm going to get it dirty."

She looked at him a long time. "It's a duvet. It washes. Bleach does wonders."

"Is that an invitation?" he asked, pushing his luck.

"No," Capri said. "I'm telling you that two babies will soon be in this bed with me."

"Oh." Clearly not an invitation, so perhaps it was best that he cut out while she wasn't completely riled with him. "Hey, I've got some runs to make. I'm going to leave Jack here for security, and Kelly here to be bedside companion—"

"Neither of which I need, thanks. What I need is peace and quiet," his darling and opinionated wife reminded him.

Seagal grinned. "And Mrs. Penny will be by soon with the best gingerbread men you've ever tasted."

"All your spies are in place, then."

"You could say that. Just lie there like a princess, and everyone will be happy."

He just needed to go root Kelly and Jack out of whatever corner they'd holed up in. Capri wasn't fooling him—she'd sent the two lovebirds off to do a little nesting. She'd probably given Kelly detailed instructions on how to seduce a man. Capri had certainly seduced the heck out of him.

And being seduced by Capri had convinced him that bachelorhood was overrated by far.

Capri raised a brow, purposefully looked at the door.

"You know," Seagal said, glancing around the bedroom they'd once shared, "I notice you don't have your usual Christmaspalooza all over the house."

She wrinkled her nose. "I've been busy."

He nodded. "I checked out the nursery. There's nothing in it but a white dresser."

"I was busy planning Christmastown. I thought I had time. I've never been on bed rest in my life."

He looked at the fireplace mantel in the room, which had Christmas cards on it but no decorations. Last year she'd twined the mantel with greenery and pine cones, setting angels at each end. "Well, there's always next year."

She lay there looking at him with those big eyes, saying nothing.

Okay, he got the message. There wasn't going to be a next year—not for the two of them. At least, not in her happy-ever-after scenario.

His little wife had no idea how much she really, really wanted him. It was going to kill him, but he was willing to wait until she figured it out.

SEAGAL WASN'T COMFORTABLE walking into his wife's flower shop, even though he'd once spent quite a bit of time hanging out at the Bridesmaids Bouquet. During their courtship, he'd liked to stop off on his breaks and chat with her. There was nothing he loved better than visiting Capri when she was surrounded by flowers. Her shop was a soft, gentle place, and it suited her.

Later, after their wedding, he'd sometimes talked her into letting him help her in the shop. He carted around boxes, unpacked things, even pushed the broom. The goal was to be with her. He would bring frosted cupcakes just to be close to her. Some men couldn't wait to get to their jobs, get away from their wives, their home lives.

He'd never been like that with Capri. She was a serene and peaceful counterpoint to his job. And his own childhood.

He had never been able to believe his luck in getting her to go out with him on a first date. Capri had asked him for a date after he and Daisy Donovan broke up, so shyly and sweetly it would have taken a coldhearted man to say no. Not that he would have said no to Capri Snow. Daisy and he had been a relationship that ran hot and cold, all fire, lots of ice, no substance.

He'd wanted to give Capri his whole world. Hot,

cold and everything in between, she was the sun in his barren existence.

"Hi," Jade Harper said when he walked in to the flower shop. Jade was Capri's trusted associate. Seagal liked the green-eyed brunette, understood why Capri trusted her with her livelihood.

But he wasn't here to trust anyone.

"How've you been, Jade?"

"Fine." She pushed a huge floral arrangement toward him. "Take this to Capri, please. It's from the Boo in the Night Society. Isn't it gorgeous?"

He stared at the pink and blue blossoms spilling from a big crystal vase. "Yes, it is."

"And this one, too, please." She waved at a silvery tabletop Christmas tree laden with tiny paper presents and a golden star in front of him. "This is from the Christmastown committee. They wanted to thank her for doing such a good job with Christmastown." Jade smiled at him. "I have a few more orders in the back, but I haven't made them up yet."

Seagal held up a hand. "Take your time. There's only so much room in my truck. I guess you have no one to do your deliveries?" He hadn't thought about it before, but it made sense. Usually Jade did them in the white van that had Bridesmaids Bouquet Floral Shop lettered on the side in big scrolling hot-pink letters.

He'd done a few deliveries for Capri. That's why the whole smuggling thing was bugging him. Capri kept an obsessive eye on her prized presentations. "You ever notice anyone hanging around here, Jade?"

"Customers." Jade looked at him. "Lots of customers. It happens at Christmas. Will you tell Capri she needs to hire another seasonal worker? Kelly said she'd come by to help, but I'm worried about the wedding we have booked, and all the Christmas orders, too." Jade smiled. "I know you're about to have twins. I hate to put another worry on the two of you. And congratulations on the babies, Seagal. I heard about it from Jack."

"He gets around." Seagal sighed. "I'll tell Capri, although she's on strict bed rest. I don't know who she could interview in a hurry."

"I'm working late every night, too," Jade said. "I won't let her down."

He glanced around the shop, looking for anything out of place. "You don't ever get anybody in here who's not a customer?"

"Nope. Everybody needs something this time of year. The shop is booming." The phone rang, and Jade went to pick it up. "Tell Capri hello for me."

Nodding, he picked up the two arrangements, heading to his truck.

"Is love in the air?" someone asked him, and he put the arrangements in the truck bed before he turned to face Justin Morant.

"Hey," Seagal said, surprised to see the rodeo champ in Bridesmaids Creek. He pounded Justin on the back with enthusiasm. "What are you doing back in town?"

"It's the holidays," Justin said, "and I'll be leaving again as fast as I can."

Seagal laughed. "I remember feeling that way."

Justin raised a brow. "Something change around here?"

"No." Seagal secured the arrangements and dusted off his hands. "It's still small-town, gossip-at-the-speed-of-light, sweet Bridesmaids Creek. I just missed it."

Justin eyed the flowers in the truck. "Looks like you missed something. Maybe not the town as much as your wife."

"You're probably right. Say hello to your folks for me, Justin. It's good to see you." He went to get into the truck, then a thought hit him. "If you've got five minutes to help me out, Capri's on complete bed rest, and Jade Harper's watching the shop for her. She had a ton of orders today and could use a deliveryman."

And a strong male, in case anything strange happened.

Justin shrugged. "Be happy to help any way I can. Heard about the twins. Congratulations."

"Who'd you hear it from?"

Justin grinned. "Everybody I've run into. Say hi to Capri for me. You sure were lucky when you roped that one."

Seagal got into his truck and pulled away.

Yeah. He'd gotten very lucky.

But then his luck had run out.

"I'M SUSPICIOUS," Capri told Kelly after Seagal left. "He's being far too attentive."

Kelly smiled and handed Capri a cup of hot tea. "He's going to be a father. Anyway, you know Seagal has always been good with detail. It's probably what moved him up so fast in the force."

"There's something else going on here," Capri said. "You don't know him like I do. Seagal never gets this focused unless there's a case."

"Isn't it possible you're his only case?" Kelly sipped at her own cup of steamy hot tea in a floral teacup. "This blackberry currant tea is fabulous."

Capri shook her head. "It's probably the pregnancy making me a little paranoid. Hormones going wild." She put a hand on her stomach. "I think I'm having a bronc buster and a cheerleader."

"Active, huh?" Kelly laughed. "Tell me again why you and Seagal decided to call it quits?"

Capri put her cup down. "I never got comfortable in the marriage, and I don't think he did, either. I always felt like he still cared for Daisy, and Seagal said I didn't trust him, and that bothered him." She thought about it, remembering. It was still pretty painful. "Daisy called the house even after we were married, always on some pretext of needing something from Seagal. She claimed they were just friends, but I knew she still cared about him. Not that I was surprised. Seagal said she hadn't wanted to break up—he did. I just happened to be the first date he had."

"But why did you marry him if you were so worried?" Kelly asked.

"I wanted him," Capri said softly. "I wanted to believe that all the late nights wouldn't make me crazy. He wanted to get promoted and moved to a different division, then got into the Rangers. I was busy taking over the flower shop. We grew apart."

"Not too apart to make babies," Kelly said, her tone gleeful. "When you found out you were pregnant, you should have realized then that Seagal was never going to let you go through with the divorce."

"I didn't want to tell him for just that reason." The memory upset Capri, which the babies seemed to notice. Inside her, they felt as if they were rolling, tumbling, fighting for space. A sudden cramp shot across her abdomen, pinching and slicing. She closed her eyes against the pain, waiting for it to pass. "Darn my brother Beau," she said after a moment. "He ratted me out."

Kelly laughed. "Good for Beau."

"I'll take care of him later." Capri leaned back against the pillow. "I know Seagal too well. There's a reason he's back in town, and it isn't all about these babies. He claims it's about the drugs in the floral arrangements, but I think there's something else. He takes a lot of phone calls when he thinks I don't notice, and his phone must get a hundred texts an hour." She sighed, wishing the cramp would pass, and forced a smile at Kelly. "Intuition. It's kind of a wife thing, I guess."

"But you're not worried about Daisy anymore now, are you?"

"No." Capri shook her head. "I think she moved on to Jack, just like you said."

"I know," Kelly said, "and it makes me want to pinch her head off."

Capri smiled. "I remember that emotion."

"So, what are you going to do now? You're not really going to go through with the divorce, are you?"

Capri could barely focus on her friend's question. The pain was getting worse; it was harder to hold back a groan.

Something was different; she knew it. "Kelly," she said, forcing her voice above a whisper but having to push against the pain, "having never experienced pregnancy I'm no expert, but I think these babies want to be here in time for Christmas."

Chapter Five

Seagal figured he'd set a new record for speed by the time he got to the hospital. He sprinted inside, leaving Jack at the curb to park the cruiser.

Capri looked pale, tired and in pain when he jogged into the room the nurse led him to. "I thought I told you to stay still," he said to his wife, trying to make light of the situation to calm his heart, which was trying to beat out of his chest.

"I listened," Capri said. "Funny how your children didn't. Maybe a case of like father, like babies."

He glanced at the doctor. "What's happening?"

Dr. Blankenship finished looking over the charts he held. "You're about to meet your children, Seagal."

Seagal's gaze locked on his wife. He'd never wanted to hold her and comfort her so badly. "This is it, lady. There's no turning back now. We're going to be parents."

Capri gave him a very slight smile. He could tell she was really hurting. "There was no turning back when I first met you, Seagal," she said, then groaned and closed her eyes.

Nurses hustled Capri onto a gurney. He followed helplessly, not sure what to do. His heart thundered. No one seemed to care whether he went in to the big room that looked like an operating room, and then suddenly, a nurse helped him into something she called a birth coach's shirt. She showed him where to wash and made him put sterile covers on his shoes.

"Are you all right?" the elderly nurse asked him.

He was pretty sure he'd know her if she'd take off her mask, but at the moment his brain was short-circuiting. "I'm fine. Is she going to be all right?"

"Your wife is going to be fine."

The nurse left him, and Seagal hung at the back of the huge room, watching everything. He didn't want to get in the way of the medical personnel; he felt so useless. Was he supposed to take pictures? He and Capri hadn't discussed his role.

Someone nudged him over to Capri's side, and told him to talk to her in soothing tones.

He wasn't usually a soothing presence for Capri. But once upon a time, he had known just the right words to say to her.

"Hey, babe."

Capri's eyes were huge in her face. He could hardly bear to see her like this. Taking her hand in his, he said, "You're the most beautiful woman I've ever known."

She made little short puffing breaths, and then suddenly she relaxed.

"A local anesthetic," the doctor explained.

They were awfully busy under the green sheet. Capri had told him he wasn't to approach the sheet in any way, so he remained by her side, letting her squeeze his fingers bloodless. He welcomed the pain; it wasn't nearly what she was going through.

"Seagal," Capri suddenly said, startling him.

"Yes?" He leaned close to hear her.

"Mrs. Penny called."

He blinked. "Can we talk to her later? I know she's one of our town's revered grapevines, but—"

Capri squeezed his fingers to shush him. She was so pale he sent a worried glance the doctor's way. Dr. Blankenship seemed busy with whatever he was doing under the green sheet thing, so Seagal looked back at Capri.

"Okay," he said, "was there something special on her mind?"

"She said you're sniffing around my flower shop." Capri's gaze was on him, accusing. "Do you think somebody close to me may be involved?"

He was on the ropes here—he could hear it in her voice. "I can't say, honey."

"You didn't tell me," Capri said.

"Keep soothing her, Mr. West. We need to keep Mom calm," a nurse said, glancing at a monitor.

He leaned close to his wife. "Let's talk about this later."

"I need to know," she said, her gaze on him, haunted.

"I don't know what you want me to say," Seagal said, "I'm simply following orders."

Capri's eyes widened. Belatedly, Seagal remembered that the night of their worst argument, he'd said the same thing. It had effectively ended their marriage.

"Capri," he said, "no one knows exactly who is involved. But this I do know. I'm about to be a dad. All I want to do is take care of you and my children."

"That's better," the nurse said, her tone approving. "Whatever you're saying, keep saying it. We need to keep your blood pressure down, Mrs. West."

"Snow," Capri said, and the nurse glanced at her. "My name is Snow."

"Now wait," Seagal said, his voice low so the nurses

and doctor couldn't hear. His blood pressure felt as if he needed someone to say soothing things to *him.* "You're still Mrs. Seagal West for another two weeks."

She closed her eyes.

"You're doing fine," the nurse said. "The doctor is almost finished prepping you, and then it will be time to meet your new babies."

Capri released his fingers. He tried to catch her fingers back but she put her hand under the covers. So he stood beside her, staring down at her pale face, wishing he knew what to tell her to make her happy, to keep her his forever.

"Okay, Capri," Dr. Blankenship said. "I'm about to make an incision. You'll only notice some tugging sensations. If you notice anything more than that, let me know, all right?"

Capri nodded. Seagal felt all the blood rush from his head.

"Get Dad a chair," Dr. Blankenship barked, and the elderly nurse led him over to the side.

"Breathe," the nurse commanded. "Doc's done this a thousand times. Capri's in the best possible hands."

Wasn't he supposed to be a fearless, tough guy?

Then why was the very idea of his wife being in pain making him weak as a kitten?

"I'm failing at being a birth coach," he told the nurse.

"We keep this chair in here for dads," the nurse said, her tone kindly. "You'll feel stronger in a bit. Don't worry. Your wife is in good hands."

She patted him on the back, then turned to stand by Capri. Seagal took another deep breath, braced himself, and went back to being there for his wife.

CAPRI KNEW THE SECOND Seagal left her side. She felt alone as soon as he'd gone, and reminded herself that she was destined to be alone in the future anyway.

Then he came back, and she felt better again.

"Are they going to be all right?" she asked.

"Of course," Seagal told her. "The babies are doing fine. You're doing fine."

"Where'd you go?"

He glanced toward the elderly nurse. She wasn't paying any attention to him. "I didn't look under the sheet, if that's what you're asking."

Capri turned her head to look at him. "I know."

"Although, didn't the sheet rule only hold when the babies were supposed to make a different exit?" He took her fingers in his, and she was glad for the warmth.

"The sheet is off-limits anyway."

"I'm good with that."

He'd agreed too quickly. She looked at her husband. "Are you all right?"

"I'm fine. Pretty eager to get started on the Dad of the Year award."

She tried to ignore what the doctor was doing. Once she'd heard *tugging sensation,* she hadn't wanted to focus on her stomach at all.

She was grateful Seagal was by her side.

"I should have told you sooner," she suddenly said, and Seagal squeezed her fingers. "You had every right to be here. And I wouldn't have wanted you to miss this."

"I knew you'd want me," Seagal said with his customary humbleness.

She had a retort ready, but then Dr. Blankenship said, "Here we are," and a baby cried out, and Capri could barely see for the sudden tears in her eyes.

"A healthy boy," Dr. Blankenship said. "A little premature, of course, but everything looks good for now." He handed the baby to a nurse, who went to suction the baby, and Capri felt Seagal take her hand in both of his.

"He sounds strong," he said.

"Like you," Capri said.

"Probably," Seagal said, and she tried not to smile.

"And here is baby sister," Dr. Blankenship said, holding up a little girl for Capri and Seagal to see before the nurse whisked the baby off.

"Oh, my gosh," Capri said, unable to help the tears that started from her eyes. "They're beautiful. Aren't they, Seagal?"

He leaned over and kissed her forehead. "Like their mother. Lucky babies."

He kissed her lips, just a brush, nothing pressuring, nothing serious. Just an acknowledgment of the moment they'd shared.

Yet Capri wished it wasn't just a moment, but forever, the way they'd once thought it would be.

"HE'S LIKE A BEAR out there," Kelly said to Capri. "He spends all his time staring in the window at the babies." She put two stuffed bears on the windowsill, one wearing a blue bow and the other a pink. "I thought Seagal was supposed to be guarding you."

"It was a ruse." Capri smiled. "Thank you for the bears."

"Oh, those are the babies' gifts. This is for you." She handed Capri a box tied with a silver ribbon. "Best-friend privilege."

Capri smiled. "Your turn is next."

"I don't know. I don't think I have a man crazy about

me like Seagal is for you. What do you mean, Seagal guarding you is a ruse?"

"He's just doing his job." She got annoyed all over again thinking about Seagal poking around in her shop looking for contraband and accomplices—as if he didn't know very well that she had control over every aspect of her shop. "In my opinion, he and whoever on the force decided I needed a bodyguard are just wrong. There are no drugs in my shop. They had to have been put in the arrangements after we put them out at Christmastown." She pulled the beautiful silver bow from the box and opened it, drawing a lovely—and very sheer—black nightie from the box. "Kelly, this is gorgeous. But don't think I don't know exactly what you're doing." She held the nightie up, examining the lovely lace strategically placed in sexy areas.

"Whoa," Seagal said, coming into the room. "If that's your idea of a hospital gown, I'm into it."

Capri stuffed it hurriedly back into its box, feeling herself blush and hoping Seagal didn't notice. "How are the babies? When are they bringing them back to me?"

"Five minutes." Seagal grinned at Kelly. "I'll have to tell Jack about your taste in nightwear."

"You think he'd approve?" Kelly asked.

"He's a live male," Seagal said. "I feel safe saying he'd approve."

"Then you two are discussing things even cop partners shouldn't be talking about," Kelly said archly. "You go right ahead and tell Jack. Maybe it'll get his mind off Daisy."

Capri watched Seagal carefully for his reaction to Daisy's name. Seagal smiled at Kelly. "You're right. There are some things partners don't need to know about."

Jack came into the hospital room at that moment, going over to kiss Capri on the cheek. "What does your partner not need to know?" Jack asked, glancing at Seagal. "Hi, Kelly."

Kelly brightened. "Hi, Jack."

"If I wanted my partner to know something, I'd tell him," Seagal said.

"That's what I thought. Locked up like Fort Knox as usual." He handed Capri a teal-and-pink-polka-dotted bag with lots of paper tissue poking out the top. "This is from Aunt Mathilda. She said she'll be by in a little while to visit. Be prepared, I think she's planning a shower for you. You caught her by surprise by giving birth a little earlier than everyone expected. It'll be a Christmas baby shower now."

"That's so sweet." Capri felt overwhelmed by her friends' kindness. She glanced at Seagal, who gazed at her with a question in his eyes. She wondered what he was thinking, because he certainly seemed focused on her. She felt sparks, as she always did around Seagal. Turning away from her husband, she opened Mathilda's gift, smiling at the tiny Christmas sleepers inside. "Now I feel like Christmas is on the way. This is all that was missing."

Seagal took one of the outfits from her, admiring the tiny red-and-white-striped outfit. "They'll look like little candy canes."

The proud look on Seagal's face nearly broke her heart. It was all Capri could do not to think about the fact that her marriage would be over in less than two weeks.

Almost on cue, Daisy Donovan walked into the room.

Chapter Six

Daisy carried a huge, gaily decorated gift bag and beamed a smile at the men in the room. Kelly glanced at Capri with a here-comes-trouble expression on her face, and Capri hoped it was just the pregnancy hormones making her imagine that both men stood a little taller as the beautiful Daisy made her way over to Capri.

"Hi, everyone," Daisy said. She handed the gift bag to Capri. "I stopped by to look at your babies, Capri. They're beautiful."

"Thank you. It's sweet of you to come by." The gift bag rested awkwardly on the bed, and Capri forced a smile to her face. She didn't dare look at Seagal—but when he sat on the bed beside her, Capri felt so much better. She smiled at her husband. "You open this one, since I opened the last two."

"Wish I'd gotten to open the sexy nightie," Seagal said, just for her ears, winking at her. Capri blinked, not certain how to respond. Daisy had gone over to chat with Jack, and Kelly looked as if she didn't quite know what to do with herself, so Capri motioned at her friend to go chat up Jack herself.

Kelly came over and sat by Capri instead.

"Baby nighties." Seagal grinned at the tiny clothes, holding up a light pink one that read Daddy's Little

Princess and a blue one that had Mommy's Little Prince lettered on the backs.

"How nice," Kelly said.

Kelly looked pea-green with misery as Jack laughed at something Daisy said.

"Look," Seagal said, his voice so soft that Capri could barely hear him, "you can't just give her the run of the field."

Kelly looked at Seagal. "What are you suggesting?"

Capri stared at her husband, curious as to the advice he was going to offer.

"Ask him out," Seagal said. "Don't you think, Capri?"

"How would I know?" She wasn't going to let on that she knew very well what Seagal meant.

"Capri asked me out on our first date," he told Kelly.

"I know." Kelly looked at Capri. "But I'm not brave like Capri."

"It was a moment of madness," Capri said.

"She wanted my body," Seagal said.

"I always wondered how you two ended up together," Daisy said, giving Capri a look that clearly was displeased as she joined their conversation.

"Ah, past history," Jack said. "Always fun."

"I'd best be going." Kelly got up. "Good to see you, Daisy. Jack. Bye, Seagal." She hugged Capri goodbye. "I'll stop back in tomorrow. When can you go home?"

"Maybe tomorrow. The babies will follow later." Capri felt anxious about leaving her babies behind.

"I'll be going, too." Jack saluted his partner. "Good going, Dad, Mom."

"I'll walk out with you, Jack," Daisy said. "Goodbye, Capri. Congratulations to both of you, Seagal." She hugged them both, Seagal longer. Capri tried not to steam, and Kelly rolled her eyes at Capri behind Daisy's head.

"Thank you for the baby gifts, Daisy." Capri made herself smile.

"I came as soon as I could." Daisy put her arm through Jack's. "Walk me to my car, Jack."

Jack raised a brow at Seagal as he walked out with Daisy.

"Well, that was interesting," Seagal said. "Let that be a lesson to both of you."

"About what?" Capri demanded.

"That men need guidance." Seagal looked innocent. "Cute outfits, though. Very thoughtful of her."

"Whatever," Capri said, feeling very disagreeable. In fact, she felt strange stirrings she recognized—and didn't want to have. "Ask Jack out, Kelly. Don't give up without a fight."

Seagal smiled at her, a slow, sexy smile that Capri tried to discourage with a frown. "What?" she demanded.

"I was just wondering if that's why you asked me out."

"What do you mean?"

Seagal turned to Kelly. "She's right. Ask him out. What's the worst that can happen? He says no."

"Exactly," Kelly said, "and that will stink."

The babies were wheeled in and Capri sat up to gaze at her children. "Look how perfect they are," she told Seagal.

"They're amazing," Kelly said. "I can't wait to be able to hold them."

"Auntie Kelly wants to hold you," Capri told the twins. "Not to mention your parents do, too."

"Do they have names?" Kelly asked. "Not to rush

you or anything, but as an aunt-in-waiting, I'd like to be able to call them something besides Baby Number One and Baby Number Two. I feel like I'm reading out of a Dr. Seuss book."

Capri looked at Seagal. "We haven't talked about it yet. Since they came early, we hadn't had a chance to debate names."

"Debate?" Seagal raised a brow.

"Do we ever have a discussion without a debate?" Capri said. "I thought it was part of your nature to dissect every detail."

"Yeah, but not baby names." Seagal grinned.

"I'll leave you two to discuss. I think the parking lot should be clear of Daisy by now. I do wish she wouldn't ride that motorcycle around everywhere," Kelly griped.

"Better than a broom," Capri said, and Seagal laughed.

"You girls are mean." He went over to look in the bassinets at his children. "I'm naming the girl Lila May."

"That's…not happening," Capri said.

"And the debate begins. Goodbye, you two. Let me know what's going on the birth certificates."

Kelly left the room, and Capri raised her brows. "Lila May sounds like a name a man picks when he wants the wife to do all the work."

Seagal shrugged. "Probably." He reached out to touch his daughter. "She's so tiny we'll have to give her a big name to compensate."

"Why are men always concerned with compensating?" Capri asked, still nettled by feeling what she recognized as jealousy. "Do you have to look so happy every time Daisy shows up wearing a short skirt and a smile for you?"

He sank back on the bed beside her. "It's an ego boost. Not a love story."

Capri sniffed. "Still."

"The babies are getting restless," Seagal said, glancing over at the bassinets. "Aren't you supposed to feed them?"

"I can't with you in the room," Capri said primly.

"Oh." Seagal nodded. "You want me to leave just when things are getting interesting."

"Breast milk is not interesting."

He looked hopeful. "There's never a time a breast isn't interesting."

Capri sighed. "Hand me Carter, Seagal, please."

He looked at her. "Carter?"

"Can you do better?"

"Sara and Carter West," Seagal said, mulling the names. "I think it'll work. Now, can we get on to the good stuff?" he said, handing her Carter.

"Go," Capri said.

"I didn't look under the sheet," he reminded her. "I promise not to look at anything you don't want me to."

It seemed mean to cast him out when he wanted so badly to be with his children. She thought about their impending divorce, and the fact that she still hadn't read Seagal the riot act about poking around her shop for signs of trafficking. "I'm not happy with you," she said.

"Daisy means nothing to me," Seagal said, reaching out to rest an arm around her shoulder. "Trust me, she didn't the day you asked me out."

Capri stared into her husband's eyes. His expression was so sincere, and it was true that Daisy threw herself at every man.

Capri had thrown herself at Seagal, too. And she'd

never regretted that, not even when they'd decided their marriage wasn't going to work out.

"This isn't as exciting as you think it is," she said. "It just involves a pump."

He grinned. "Sounding kinkier all the time, babe."

"THE THING YOU HAVE to understand," Seagal told Capri an hour later as he stretched out on the rollaway the nurse had brought in for him, "is that even if I could leave you on your own, I wouldn't."

The babies had been taken back to the nursery. They weren't allowed to be out of preemie care for very long, just long enough to let Capri express some breast milk while they were in the room. Then the nurses used her milk in the feeding tubes. Capri longed for the time when she could actually hold the babies to her breast.

"What do you mean?" she asked Seagal, distracted by the sight of her husband stretched out on the bed, distracted by thinking about her babies, and distracted in general.

"I'm with you for two reasons. One, a man needs his children. Two, I'm protecting you. Even if you were fully ambulatory and capable, there are outstanding reasons you need me."

Capri thought about bursting her husband's bubble but decided against it. "I know you were snooping around in my shop, Seagal. It's hard to trust you when I know you either don't trust me, or don't think I would know if someone was using my shop as a front for some kind of nefarious operation. I really don't appreciate it." She looked over the bed rail at him, annoyed. "So, did you find anything?"

He shook his head. "There's nothing there. I think the floral arrangements were a random placement opportunity. I mean, the operation was planned to a T, but it was small-time and hardly professional, where something more sinister would be. I think we have a case of inside activity rearing its ugly head in Bridesmaids Creek."

"You think local people are involved and that it wasn't an outside thing?"

"Right. At first I was afraid we might have a cartel situation going on, or a developing gang. Because of the timing, I'm beginning to suspect that it was opportunistic because of the holidays. Only locals would know our traditions here." He looked thoughtful. "As you know, not everybody in Bridesmaids Creek has the town's best interests at heart. There are people here who don't love the BC legend like most of us do."

"You left Bridesmaids Creek. I don't remember you claiming to love it before."

"I always loved the town and its people. I wanted to move up, and that meant working in other departments in other places." He looked thoughtful. "Opportunities to get promoted don't come along all the time. I had to take advantage of what came my way."

It was true. She didn't blame him for that. But there were moments and words she remembered that were painful.

"I know you think I left you alone so much because I didn't care about you, Capri. That was never the case."

"I wanted to believe it wasn't," she said softly.

"Believe it," Seagal said, his words clipped. "Maybe the timing wasn't good."

"Probably not." Capri sighed. The nights had been long. She'd been busy trying to take over her grandmother's shop. "We didn't talk a lot."

He didn't say anything for a moment. "We might have gotten married too soon."

After he and Daisy had broken up, were the unspoken words. Capri turned her head on her pillow, and put a hand on her stomach where the stitches tugged painfully. "Maybe."

"It felt right at the time."

Capri blinked away a tear. "I know."

Things hadn't worked out. It wouldn't matter in two weeks. They'd walk into the courthouse, talk to a judge, sign some papers and walk away with the babies as the only things that bound them.

She didn't want to think about it.

"Anyway, we have two beautiful children," Seagal said.

She clicked out the light overhead, casting the room into darkness.

"Capri?"

"Yes?" She lay still, listening.

"There was never another woman for me after our marriage."

She swallowed. "I know."

"What I'm trying to say is that I never thought about anybody else after you asked me out. I was gone a lot, but it was always about my job."

She knew he was telling the truth. Seagal was an honorable man. He would never have cheated on her.

Even if he had still been in love with another woman. And that bothered her more than she could say.

TWO DAYS LATER, Seagal took Capri home. "Home sweet home," he said.

"It's not a sweet home without the babies," Capri said.

"They'll be here soon enough. They just need a few

more days to acclimate." Seagal helped Capri walk inside, smiling when she gasped at the sight of all the flower arrangements and fruit baskets piled in the living room. He'd crowded many of the gifts into the formal room, on top of the stuffed floral sofa, and near the white-mantled fireplace.

Then Capri saw he'd put up a Christmas tree, and her eyes widened with delight—just as he'd hoped. "Oh, Seagal! Thank you!"

She moved slowly to the fireplace, where he'd hung stockings her mother had brought over with the babies' names on them. "These are darling! Carter and Sara," she murmured, looking at the beautiful gilt-lettered red velvet stockings.

"Your mom came by," Seagal said. "She brought the stockings, helped me decorate the tree, put the wreaths on the doors. I was doing all right by myself, but I was glad when the cavalry arrived."

Capri smiled. "I don't know when you had time to do this."

"I'm learning to be very organized." He eased her toward her bedroom, but she glimpsed the tiny presents under the tree before he could.

"What are those?"

"Those are from Santa. They're for the babies. Come on, Mama, let's get you to bed. Doctor's orders."

"What are they?" she asked, eying the tiny blue-and-pink-wrapped packages. There were three of them, one with a blue bow, one with pink and one with silver.

"Santa didn't tell me."

"You are Santa," she said. "What did you buy the children?"

He grinned. "Footballs."

She stared at him. "Footballs."

"What else does a dad get his brand-new babies? I can't wait for them to come home so they can open them."

"They won't open them, Seagal."

"It doesn't matter. They'll be here for them when they get home, and then they'll be here when the babies are ready to play with me."

Capri's expressions was adorably confused. "Footballs."

"Sure. A pink one for Sara and a regular one for Carter."

"Nerf or stuffed?"

"Stuffed. Nice and soft, for their first catches." He grinned. "Don't feel left out. I got you one, too. But I'm not telling you what color yours is."

She glanced toward her box. "You got me a football."

"Was there something you would rather have had?"

She shook her head. "I guess a football is fine."

"Good. Merry Christmas. Now, on to bed." He herded her toward the hallway that led to the bedroom, but she kept glancing back toward the tree.

"It's beautiful, Seagal. Thank you so much for doing that. I didn't feel like it was Christmas without the tree up. And I just ran out of time before I could get it put up."

"It's not like you didn't have anything better to do." He finally got her into the hall—but he didn't get her into her bedroom before she'd spied that the door to the nursery was closed.

"Why is that door shut?" Capri demanded.

"To keep the warm air out here in the hall," Seagal said, knowing very well his quick-thinking wife wasn't going to buy that lame excuse.

She went to the nursery, pushing open the door. "Oh, my goodness!"

It was a baby wonderland, if he did say so himself. He waited for Capri's reaction to the amazing nursery that had bloomed in her absence.

"Did you do all this?" she asked, moving into the room, gently running her hands over the two new white cribs.

"The nursery I cannot take credit for. I wouldn't know the first thing to buy babies."

"Footballs," she said, smiling, moving to touch the soft blankets in each crib and the mobiles hanging overhead.

"Okay, I wouldn't know the first *practical* thing to buy babies. Mrs. Penny and your mother had a little baby shower in here. I guess that's what you'd call it. The folks from the Boo in the Night Society, the Honeymoon Hotel, the Wedding Diner, Mosey Montgomery's Etiquette and Cotillion, the Wed & Bed B&B, and even the sheriff's Murder, He Votes club came by. It was a houseful." He smiled. "The Murder, He Votes guys put together the cribs and hung the curtains, fixed mobiles and baby swings. The heavy lifting."

He watched his wife continue to walk around the room, examining each bit of baby paraphernalia with a smile. It was good to see Capri happy. Ever since he'd come back to town and figured out a way to move into the house with her, it seemed she hadn't smiled much. Of course, she hadn't felt much like smiling, maybe—she'd once said she felt as if she'd swallowed a Christmas turkey—and she'd been anxious about the babies once the doctor put her on bed rest.

It was good to see her smile.

"The ladies weren't sure what colors you wanted.

They left receipts for everything, in case you wanted to swap any of the—"

"It's perfect." She turned to him, her eyes shining. "Nothing will need to be swapped. I'm so grateful for all of our friends."

He started when she said *our*. He couldn't remember Capri speaking of them as an "our" in the past couple of weeks. It felt good.

But he didn't want to spook her, so he merely said, "If I don't get you in bed, I'm going to get in trouble with Doc."

She looked around the nursery one last time. "Thank you, Seagal. Even though you're not admitting that you did any of this, I'm pretty sure you had a hand in it."

He warmed under her appreciation. "Well, I did take a lot of pictures. Your mother is going to start a baby photo album for you."

Capri smiled. "Thank you. For everything."

He nodded. "You're welcome."

She didn't say anything else as she walked past him down the hall. He glanced around the nursery one last time, taking in all the amazing and beautiful things their friends had bought for the babies.

He so badly wanted to be here every night of the babies' lives, watching over them, taking care of them.

He turned off the light and closed the door.

Chapter Seven

When the babies finally came home two days before Christmas, Seagal was amazed by how much different the house felt. The house literally *changed.*

"You can't believe the difference," he told Jack. "It's like the house is magical now or something. It's beautiful. I thought it would be panic and craziness—and it is—but mostly, it just feels so awesome."

Jack raised a beer to him in the Wedding Diner. "Makes you think, doesn't it?"

Seagal wasn't sure he'd been doing much thinking. Right now he was more into *feeling.* With the babies and Capri, everything was open and new and exciting. "The divorce will be final the day after Christmas. Yes, the court does have office hours that day, despite the holiday season. I'm going to have to face a Grinch in a black robe and sign off from my marriage."

Jack stared at him. "You're going through with it?"

"Do I have a choice?"

"I don't know." Jack looked at him. "Do you?"

"I don't think so. My wife hasn't indicated there's to be a change in plans."

"You may have to help her with that."

Seagal winced. "Capri isn't easily swayed. For instance, she threw me out for the afternoon. She told me that she didn't need a bodyguard, she needed sleep, and while the babies were napping she was going to sleep like a rock, and I was going to leave the house or she was going to sue the department for harassment."

Jack laughed. "Did she really threaten to call the chief? And the sheriff?"

"I don't think it was an idle threat." Seagal sipped his beer. "How am I supposed to change her mind?" He'd done everything he knew how to do, which was nothing more than continue being her husband. "I love her so much. I just don't think Capri feels the same way."

"Oh, I think she does." Jack glanced around the pink-and-white walls of the Wedding Diner. "Kelly says she thinks Capri loves you madly. But things were kind of rocky from the beginning. At least that's what Kelly says."

Seagal blinked. "What else does Kelly say?"

"That Capri feels like she stole you from Daisy."

"That's dumb."

"And that you never got over Daisy."

"That's even dumber," Seagal said. "If I wanted to be with Daisy, I would be."

"You can't really tell that to a woman. They don't understand the difference between attraction and true love."

Seagal shook his head. "I never thought about Daisy again after Capri asked me out. That's the truth."

"I know," Jack said. "But women don't really get that."

Seagal pondered the information for a moment. "It shouldn't matter. I'm a married dad. My 'hot' quotient for the ladies has hit rock bottom."

"Dude," Jack said with a laugh, "if anything, it's made you even more attractive to the ladies. They love a steady-Eddie kind of guy." He shrugged. "Deep down, wives know this stuff. It gets to them. They don't like feeling less attractive to the opposite sex than their husbands are."

"This is the most existential crap I've ever heard you spout," Seagal said. "You're actually starting to bring me down. Your job is to make me feel better, give me hope, not talk a bunch of philosophical egghead nonsense."

"It's true," Jack said. "Ask her."

Seagal drank his beer, waved for another. "You want me to go home, ask Capri if she feels I've got more options with the opposite sex than she does, and that will fix my marriage."

"I'm saying try to see it from the chick's point of view."

Seagal looked at his partner. "Look. First thing, if I called Capri a chick, she'd hand me my head. I'm just treading water with her."

"All right. Listen, just take on some of the Venus angle, okay? Women think differently than we do. They worry about stuff we never dream they'd worry about. Do I have to draw you a diagram?"

"Yes," Seagal said.

Jack shook his head. "Right now I can assure you Capri is worried about baby weight. Lumps and bumps. Leaking breasts."

"I wish I could see leaking breasts," Seagal said morosely. "Capri does not let me in the room when she's nursing. If I go in there, she wraps up like a mummy."

Jack laughed. "Too much info. Why is your skull so thick?"

"I don't know." He guessed it was, because Jack seemed to get it and Seagal sure didn't. "I've got to go.

I've got a cruiser going around the house every five minutes while I'm gone, and if Capri looks out the window and sees it, I'm toast. She's fed up with the case. She says she wants her life back, and the best way to make that happen is to get me out of the house."

Jack nodded. "Probably right."

"Thanks. Help me some more, why don't you." He tossed tip money on the table.

"What if there's never a lead in the case?" Jack asked. "Your divorce is final soon and you're out on your ear. Then what?"

Seagal knew the pressure was on. Christmas Day was his last day to be under the same roof with Capri and the children—she'd made no bones about it. "I have a pretty good idea what's happened. It's a local job—some of the Bridesmaids Creek loose cannons have too much time on their hands. They were making a handoff and decided Christmastown was the best place to do it. And there were Capri's big, beautiful Christmas arrangements, with vases big enough to hold stash."

"How do you know this?" Jack asked.

"Daisy sort of told me." Seagal leaned back in the pink vinyl booth. "When she came to the hospital to see Capri, I looked out the window as she left. She rode off on the back of Taylor Kinsler's motorcycle."

"Oh, that's bad," Jack said. "Nothing good can come of that."

"Nope. He's been spoiling to get in trouble for years. Things haven't gone well for him at rodeo, mainly because he doesn't like to work hard, which is a shame because his father, Judge Kinsler, is one of the hardest-working men I've ever known. I heard through the grapevine that Taylor picked up a bit of a weed problem when he was on the circuit. Probably thought it made him look cool to the ladies." Seagal shrugged. "Him and his boys are trouble, always have been."

"The Bad." Jack nodded. "I remember when Taylor and his friends called themselves the Bad in high school. They loved having a bad rep. Even in football, they wanted to make a blood sport out of it. It wasn't about winning for the team—it was about who they could hurt."

Seagal nodded. "I guess nothing's changed, except sometimes bad kids grow up to be criminals. It's a slippery slope."

"And Daisy's mixed up with them?"

Seagal shrugged. "Daisy likes all the guys. You know that."

"Yeah, but she's never been bad. She's more like—"

"Edgy." Seagal got up from the booth. "I can't worry about Daisy. She's a tough girl—she can take care of herself."

"Shame. All that beauty and an angel face going down the road to nowhere."

"Yeah, but it's not your problem, either. Unless you're into bad girls. I've got to head back. It's one of my last nights at the hacienda. I'm praying for a miracle, or I'll be in Judge Kinsler's court. This Santa's probably going to be sent right out on my sleigh, unless my wife experiences some kind of epiphany."

"Remember what I said," Jack called after him. "Women are different from men!"

Seagal waved as he absorbed Jack's nonsensical advice. Of course women were different from men—Jack was a softhearted knucklehead. And not as wily with women as he thought, or he'd have figured out that Kelly was all about him.

On the other hand, Seagal would take any advice if it would win his wife back. It was the only Christmas gift he wanted.

AN HOUR LATER, Seagal was still giving Capri space. He'd texted her once, and she'd texted back not to rush to return. That sounded like wife code for "I'm really enjoying the peace and quiet," so he drove around Bridesmaids Creek's courthouse another time, looking at the bright Christmas lights and decorations around the square.

Wasn't the season supposed to be about hope, about miracles?

He parked his truck across from Capri's shop and shut the engine off. Though it was dark outside, he had a fairly good view of her store. There were lights on under the pink-and-white-striped awnings that most shops had over their storefronts. He remembered Capri had ordered the new awning when she took over her grandmother's florist shop—it was the one thing she'd changed.

She'd said there was no reason to change what was working.

Not long after that, Capri had said she thought it would be better if they separated. He'd been working in Dallas, polishing his résumé and putting in some extra training hours.

She'd gone from an assistant in the Bridesmaids Bouquet shop to owner and manager when her grandmother had died. He knew things had been tough for her. He'd agreed to the separation, figuring maybe she'd feel better in time. Months had passed, and still she didn't call—though he hoped desperately that she would. Capri had taken the lead in the beginning of their relationship; it had stood to reason he'd be in good shape if he let her take the lead when she'd processed whatever she was going through.

But she never called.

Seagal leaned back, glancing around the square. He'd missed it here, more than he realized. Last Christmas he'd been gone most of the holiday season. Same thing this year, until he'd heard about the drug ring. Capri's shop had come up as a possible place the drugs were being hidden—and then her brother, Beau, had called, dropping the earth-shattering bomb on him that he was going to be a dad.

Seagal had requested a transfer with lightning speed—and bent every department ear he could find about letting him be assigned to his wife.

Maybe he'd made matters worse.

Sudden tapping at his window startled him. He rolled down the window to glare at Daisy.

"What are you doing out at this hour?" he demanded.

She laughed. "Is eight o'clock late in your world now, Seagal?"

He wasn't going to fall for her obvious reference to his not-wild lifestyle. "What can I do for you, Daze?"

Daisy's smile was sweet, angelic. Just like Jack had said. Only, Jack was stupid. *And I'm not.*

"Get tired of changing diapers?" she asked. "Is that why you're sitting here alone in the dark?"

"I doubt I'll ever tire of changing diapers. Good times, as far as I'm concerned." It was the truth. He loved spending time with his daughter and his son. Diapers were no big deal—just part of taking care of babies. He glanced over at her ride to change the subject. "Nice bike."

"Yeah." She glanced at her super-hot-pink motorcycle with pride. "A girl's gotta have wheels."

"I guess." He wouldn't classify those as just any old wheels. "I'm going to have to shove off."

Daisy looked at him, full-on sex appeal in her tight black rider duds. She hadn't worn a helmet. Her long brown hair was tousled and sexy from the wind. She looked wild and free, and he got why the guys dug her—he had, too, once upon a time.

Before he'd realized he could actually have Capri Snow, the smartest, cutest, most uptight girl in the town.

"I'm glad you came back to Bridesmaids Creek, Seagal."

"Don't see why you'd care, Daisy."

She shrugged. "You're a nice guy. There aren't a lot of men like you around."

This conversation was starting to sound a bit dangerous, like it might be all about stroking his ego. He didn't have an ego these days; it was totally invested in Capri and his kids. "Plenty of nice guys. Though I hear you're not always spending your time with the best."

She frowned. "What do you mean?"

"Saw you ride off the other night with Taylor Kinsler," he said matter-of-factly.

Her frown turned into a sexy smile. "Jealous, Seagal?"

He started to say no, not by a long shot, but she leaned over and kissed him on the lips. Seagal drew back as if he'd been struck by a snake. "Not cool, Daze," he said, started his engine, and drove away.

"AND THEN SHE KISSED HIM," Mrs. Penny said, "right on the mouth."

Capri blinked. "Are you sure it was Seagal?"

That was a dumb question, and she knew it. Nobody drove a truck like Seagal's. She wasn't surprised he was still staking out her store, either. He was determined the drugs were being trafficked through her shop, no matter how many times she told him it was impossible.

Mathilda nodded. "I could see clear as anything with the new streetlights. The only reason I'm telling you, Capri, is so you'll know that Seagal took off like the wind immediately. Daisy would have had to throw herself into the truck bed to catch him."

The two women sat in the formal room, in front of the pretty Christmas tree Seagal and her mother had decorated. The colored lights glowed softly, catching against the silver and gold ornaments. She and Mathilda were going over the Christmastown event, trying to figure out what could be improved for next year.

"It doesn't matter." Capri didn't want it to matter, but her heart ached. She had two beautiful children; she was a mom. There was no time in her life for stressing about Daisy Donovan anymore.

"You know how she is," Mathilda said. "She's always been fast."

Seagal had once loved fast. Capri sighed. "I was never fast. Sexy is not what men see in me."

"True," Mathilda said, with her customary forthrightness. "I think Seagal sees something he likes better."

Capri considered her husband as she looked around her beautiful formal room. "Sometimes I don't think we were really all that well-suited. He hated this sofa, for example, and I loved it."

Mathilda smiled at the flowery, feminine sofa. "Men

don't care about living rooms. The den is usually their cave. Wherever the television remote is."

Capri smiled. "He did enjoy our den. Lots of leather and wood. I told him to decorate that room any way he liked, and he did. Iron stuff. Manly things."

"Exactly." Mathilda nodded. "Anyway, don't think about this. I just didn't want you to be surprised when Seagal tells you about Daisy."

Shocked, she looked at her planning partner. "You think he'll tell me?"

"Sure. Seagal isn't going to want you to hear it from anyone else, least of all Daisy."

"Oh." Capri pondered that. "I guess you're right."

"I am. He's going to want his conscience clean. He wants to keep his marriage," Mathilda said simply. "The best way to do that is not to have any secrets."

"But he wouldn't admit he was staking out my shop," Capri said, and Mathilda said, "What?"

"Never mind." Capri sighed.

"He's staking out your shop? Is that what he was doing parked across the street?"

"It was just an expression." If there was an investigation under way, Seagal wouldn't want the details out. It would get him in all kinds of hot water with the department. And Mrs. Penny, bless her, was the town telephone. "I have no idea why he was parked by the courthouse."

"You have those two darling babies to think of," Mathilda said. "I was married for fifty-four years. Divorce is hard on the kids, and hard on you, too. Not that it's any of my business," she said, "but I wouldn't give up on my marriage just because of Daisy."

"It's not quite like that," Capri murmured.

"Well, it's none of my business." Mathilda gave her

a gentle smile. "I imagine you'll want to give up your position on the committee for the annual Bridesmaids Creek swim. You've got a lot on your hands."

Capri shook her head. "I'll be fine. I want to stay busy." Part of living in Bridesmaids Creek was trying to benefit the town. The town meant a lot to her. She'd been born here, raised here, knew most of the people. She cared about what the citizens of Bridesmaids Creek cared about—they pulled together through thick and thin.

"What about the charity race at Best Man's Fork? You'll surely not want to co-chair that, too?"

Capri laughed. "I know what you're trying to do. You're trying to say I have too much to do, now that I'm a mom. That I should give up my committees. The thing is, my grandmother had four children and held these positions for years. I plan to do the same."

"Of course, your grandmother had her children one at a time," Mathilda pointed out. "I've got to think it's easier to be a mom one baby at a time. Especially if you really think you're determined to be a single mom."

"I'll be fine." She'd have to be.

"People will still order their flowers for all their events at your shop if you don't sit on every committee in town."

"I know." If there was still a shop after Seagal finished poking around in it. The thought that drugs were being run through her store—it was ludicrous.

But if there were, she feared people wouldn't want to patronize her store anymore. Gossip would swirl for years. Illegal activity would make her shop infamous.

She was scared. Her shop was her livelihood.

"I need my store," Capri said, thinking about the

case Seagal was working on. Why had he been staking out her store? Had something happened? Did he know something he wasn't telling her?

It wouldn't be the first time.

Chapter Eight

Capri sat in her nightgown, staring at the beautiful Christmas tree, feeling the holiday spirit surround her despite the anxiety Mrs. Penny's visit had inadvertently stirred inside her—until Seagal burst through the front door.

She stared at her husband.

"You don't look so good," Capri said. "What happened?"

He sat next to her on the flowery sofa. "I ran into Daisy Donovan tonight."

She blinked. "Is that why you look like you've run through a wind tunnel?"

"I think I probably always look this way." He turned toward her. "There was some lip action involved, and it didn't mean anything, and I don't want you to think it did."

Capri looked at Seagal. "I already heard."

"Oh." His face fell. "That's the one thing about Bridesmaids Creek I don't like. Gossip runs faster than an electrical current." He drew a deep breath. "So, who told you?"

"Mrs. Penny."

"So the whole town will know by morning."

"I doubt it this time." Capri got up. "I'm going to check on the babies."

"Wait." He didn't speak until she turned to face him. "It meant nothing."

"We've been separated for months, Seagal. It doesn't matter."

His expression didn't change. Capri realized that was one thing about her husband the cop—he'd always been good at schooling his emotions, and she'd never known exactly what he was thinking. She looked at Seagal for a long moment, her heart aching. "Do you want to tell me why you were sitting outside my store?"

"What does that matter?"

"It matters," Capri said, amazed that Seagal wouldn't know this.

"That matters, and Daisy kissing me doesn't?"

She nodded.

"I was just sitting there, Capri. Oh, you think I was staking out your shop."

She didn't say anything.

"You're mad about this case, aren't you?"

"Of course I am. No matter how many times I try to tell you that there's no way drugs ever went through my store, you don't believe me." Capri got more upset just thinking about it. "And I did see the squad car go by several times, by the way. I know that was your doing. But you weren't going to tell me that, either."

He shook his head. "I can't believe you're mad about the case, and not Daisy."

"I might be tomorrow. Give me time. It's just that all this other stuff crowds it out. I think I'd rather deal with Daisy than with you not believing me."

"Capri, you don't know how the drugs are being transported or where they're being hidden."

"They are not in my store," Capri said.

"Maybe you're right," Seagal said, "but they were in your arrangements. That means someone was keeping an eye on you, at least enough to know when you'd be making your deliveries."

"It's dumb, Seagal," Capri said. "The whole thing was a coincidence."

He considered that. "Possibly. But not usually with drugs. People generally aren't very coincidental about where they hide stuff that's worth five thousand dollars."

Capri blinked. "That much?"

He nodded. "Why do you think I'm here? Because somebody stuffed a few joints in a flowerpot?"

"I don't know. I thought…I thought you were just being your typical overanalytical, overprotective self."

Seagal stared at her. "Are you saying I'm no fun?"

"*Fun* is not a word I would use to describe you."

"You think our marriage wasn't fun?"

He sounded either perplexed or astounded. "Not when you were being super-cop," Capri said. "I understand it's your job, but you could be a bit overbearing. I loved you, in spite of it, but then I began to realize your life was all about something that had nothing to do with me. And it's the reason you're here. You wouldn't have come back to me if there hadn't been a case in my shop."

Seagal stared as his wife exited the room. He turned to look at the Christmas tree and the pretty colored lights. There was a gold star on top, and tons of silvery beads twining through the branches. He'd spent hours trying to get the tree right to surprise Capri when she came home from the hospital.

But she thought she was just a case to him.

Christmas Eve for the floral business—at least in Capri's shop in Bridesmaids Creek—was busy until at least noon, every year. People wanted last-minute gifts to take to the in-laws, and last-minute deliveries of arrangements, especially if someone hadn't gotten to the end of their shopping list.

She'd dumped most of the work over the holidays on Jade and Kelly, but, wanting to make certain that every last detail was seen to before the shop closed for Christmas, Capri decided to ask Mathilda Penny to watch the babies for a couple of hours while she went to see if there was anything she could do to help.

That meant slipping out past Jack, the ever-present bodyguard. After she'd told Seagal he was overbearing, she'd found him gone this morning. Jack sat in her kitchen, munching on a bagel and sipping hot coffee.

She hadn't batted an eye. She'd said good-morning and gone to check on the babies.

Now Jack sat outside in the cold, keeping an eye on things, probably bored stiff. Seagal was carrying this whole thing too far, in her opinion, but that was Seagal. He carried cop work past the point where normal people would give up.

"Jack," Capri said, "I'm going to the shop. If you follow me or tell Seagal, I will tell Kelly that you snore and that you have a fetish for garlic."

He blinked. "Seagal will kill me."

She nodded. "That sounds like a personal problem to me, to use one of Seagal's favorite and irritating expressions."

"Capri, I just don't think this is a good idea. Something tells me it's not. I get these tickles—"

"You'll really get a tickle if you rat me out."

He appeared to consider his options. "Can you be

gone for only an hour? And keep your cell phone on you so I can text you if Seagal's coming back? I don't think I have to tell you that Seagal will be mad at both of us."

"The good part about that is that I'm getting a divorce from Seagal in two days, and you're not, partner."

"I don't think you really want a divorce, Capri."

She thought about Daisy kissing Seagal, felt a flashing knife stab her heart. "Maybe I don't, but I know it's for the best. Seagal married me before he really had a chance to think it through."

"Yeah, because he couldn't believe the hottest girl he'd ever laid eyes on had asked him out," Jack said. "And after he saw you at the annual Bridesmaids Creek swim, he was determined to have you. It was the bikini. Seagal said he'd never realized how fast a red bikini could blow his mind. He was talking about the bikini, but he fell for the lady wearing it, that much was obvious."

She hesitated. "Did he really say that?"

"I'm his partner. I hear everything. I don't have to make stuff up, Capri."

It was almost too good to be true. Her heart wanted to hear all this so badly. "Seagal never said he thought I was hot."

Jack laughed. "Capri, do you really think Seagal would settle for a chick who wasn't hot?"

"You've got to stop saying *chick,*" Capri said, "before some woman slaps you silly."

"I've heard that," Jack said. "I'll wait until it happens. I like living dangerously." He looked at her with a curious expression. "Didn't Seagal ever tell you that your red bikini sent the flag up his flagpole?"

She shook her head. "No."

"Well, it's Seagal. He's…like John Wayne. I've been

his partner for a long time, until he got into the Rangers. You sit in a car with someone for a few years, several hours a day, you know what they're thinking before they say it." He thought for a minute. "In fact, I knew he loved you before he even told me. Or you. It's probably a toss-up if he told me or you first that he loved you, but I knew it before he figured it out himself. He's a bit slow where women are concerned, don't you think?"

Capri's breath stilled. "I never thought so."

"Yeah. Pretty much he's slow. That's why he dated Daisy. She was willing to do the work as far as asking him out and stuff."

"I asked him out on our first date."

"Yeah," Jack said, "and the shock made him giddy as a boy at the State Fair. He never saw that coming. He couldn't talk about anything else for three days. Believe me," Jack said, "trapped in a cruiser with Seagal yakking about the hottest chick in the county is not pleasant." He sighed. "In fact, now that I think about it, Seagal's focus is exactly what makes him perfect for the Rangers. God, he's a pain in the butt."

That much Jack had right. The rest of it she couldn't say. How much was Jack building Seagal up to her, and how much was truth? "I'm going now. Do not tell Seagal I've left."

"I'm going to have to leave Bridesmaids Creek," Jack said. "I'll drop you a line from whatever outback I have to hide in."

She smiled. "Your aunt came in the back door. She's busy with the babies. You don't have to sit out here, Jack."

"I think I saw someone had put some cupcakes under a glass dome in the kitchen," Jack said hopefully.

"And your darling aunt just brought over a half turkey breast and all the sides for Christmas Eve dinner. Help yourself." She walked down the steps.

"Isn't that for your and Seagal's Christmas dinner?"

She waved a hand at Jack and kept walking. He was the partner—he ought to know better than anyone that there was no need to pretend that there was going to be a Christmas for her and Seagal.

SEAGAL COULDN'T BELIEVE his eyes when he saw his delicate wife go into her store. Today of all days he'd needed her to stay put. "Darn, Jack," he muttered. He put the binoculars back up to his eyes, watching the loading area. Nothing seemed out of place. Yet the department had been tipped off that today was the day for a "delivery"—something that had been mentioned directly by Taylor Kinsler to an undercover cop posing as a buyer.

According to Kinsler, Capri's shop was perfect because the fragrance of the flowers covered up the smell of something more pungent.

And the fact that Capri's husband was a Ranger was even better, Kinsler had said. No one would suspect them of running any drugs through a shop owned by a cop's wife.

It made Seagal's blood boil.

No one knew better than he did how hard Capri had worked in her shop, wanting it to be a place her grandmother would be proud of. Capri had loved her grandmother with all her heart, and when she'd been left the business, Capri had taken it over with appreciative enthusiasm. In some ways, working there made her feel close to her grandmother.

Capri knew that the business had kept their family going through the hard times. Capri had gone to college, thanks to the shop. Capri's mother had worked there, too, but she hadn't loved it like Capri. His wife had so much talent with making things beautiful.

She made his life beautiful.

And those babies just knocked him to his knees. In his mind, Capri's beauty went all the way down to her soul.

It tore him up that her shop was being used for illegal purposes. She'd be heartbroken.

He'd save her that if he could.

It was going to take vigilance to stamp out this operation. Seagal moved the binocs to his eyes again, watching every movement behind the plate-glass windows beneath the cheery awning. No one would think the charming store hid contraband. Customers went inside, wrapped in their warm coats to ward off the chilly temperature outside, and came out with smiles on their faces, carrying armfuls of flowers or pots of poinsettias.

He wished Capri hadn't decided to work today. But he should have figured she would—her customers meant too much to her to leave them without her careful eye on their Christmas arrangements and gifts.

He loved that about her.

In fact, he loved everything about his wife.

Suddenly, screams erupted from the flower shop. It sounded as if they were coming from the loading area. Seagal took off running, his heart in his throat.

Chapter Nine

Capri held the broom over the stranger's head, prepared to whack him to kingdom come if he so much as moved. The man lay on the shop floor, looking as though he was going to have a pretty good headache from Jade whacking him with a big glass vase.

"Call the police, Jade," Capri said.

"Wouldn't it be faster to call your husband?"

"Call 911!" Capri said. "If Seagal comes, he might kill this unfortunate thug, especially if he finds out he threatened me."

She searched the man's pockets, pulling out a knife, and a small gun. "I know what this is," she said. "It's cop-issue. This isn't good."

She kept one eye on their prisoner while Jade talked to a dispatcher. But she wasn't shocked when Seagal practically tore the glass door off its hinges. In fact, she'd have been more shocked if he hadn't materialized like Super Ranger. "What took you so long?"

Seagal grunted, turned the guy over with his boot. "Nice goose egg. Your work?"

"Jade's." She decided to leave out the detail that Jade had snuck up behind the man while he was threatening Capri.

Seagal cuffed the man, then radioed for an ambulance and backup. "Just in case," he told Capri.

"Of course. I guess you'll want me to close the shop?"

He looked at his wife. "I asked you not to move from the house, even had a bodyguard posted on you, and here you are. Would you close the shop if I asked you to?"

"I just figured," Capri said stiffly, "that the little men with the yellow caution tape and chalk outlines might show up sooner than later. I figured they work best in a non-crowded environment, and that they like their crime area kept sacrosanct from Christmas shoppers spreading yuletide cheer."

He didn't smile, even though he wanted to. "Do you know where the drugs are?"

"He didn't say anything about drugs," Capri said. "He told me to close the store early. Apparently I did last year, and since I wasn't closing early today, it was messing up his schedule. I didn't close the store early last year, did I, Seagal?"

He smiled. "I think we might have closed it about thirty minutes or so early."

She frowned for a moment, thinking, which he thought was darling. "Ohh. That's right. I did close early."

"We thought it was best not to scandalize the shoppers," Seagal reminded her.

She blushed the color of Christmas punch. "They've been planning this caper for a year?"

He shrugged. "We'll know when big boy wakes up." He gave the prone man another nudge with his boot just as the ambulance and backup arrived. "After you give your statement, could I talk you into going home?

I'll sweep and lock up. I'm sure Jack's about to have a nervous breakdown. What did you bribe him with?"

"Not much," Capri said. "Just some food."

Seagal sighed. "And his aunt is there, watching the babies? She brought goodies, I'm sure?"

Capri nodded. "He's probably eating our Christmas dinner right now."

He wasn't surprised. Local cops filled the store, working the crime scene, taking Jade's statement, looking for contraband.

"Check this out, Seagal," someone said, dragging a huge pot decorated with ghosts and pumpkins and bats from under the counter.

"Not Christmas-friendly," Seagal said to Capri. "That I didn't expect."

She stared at the pot. "I never looked twice at that."

"Because it's not Halloween. No one would be looking at fall decor."

"Decor, even," Capri said. "You're picking up some decorating lingo."

"That's right," Seagal said, his tone slightly amused. "Take her statement so she can go," he told an officer. "Her children called. They want their mother to come home to read them *The Night Before Christmas*."

"I believe that's the father's job," Capri said.

"Really?" Seagal stepped a bit closer. "Am I being invited?"

Capri met his eyes. She glanced at the thug being taken off on a stretcher, and the uniforms crowding her small shop. "Consider yourself invited."

He nodded, his heart lifting with hope. "Tell the twins Daddy will be there after he finishes with the holiday mischief. I have a few details to wrap up."

Capri went to Jade, offering to drive her home. Jade

said she was fine, and Capri told her to get her coat. She hung a *Closed for the Holidays* wreath on the front door, then handed Seagal the key to the shop. "Lock up, please. Should I send Jack home?"

Seagal nodded. "Tell him I said to go live it up on my dime. Early Christmas gift."

Capri nodded, and as he watched her leave the store to walk Jade to her car, Seagal thought how lucky he was to be married to the hottest woman he'd ever laid eyes on.

She's all I want for Christmas, Santa. Sexy mama and my two little blessings—what more could a man ask for?

CAPRI LIT SOME CANDLES—not enough to be overtly romantic, but enough to lend an air of home and comfort.

She'd been so relieved when Seagal had burst into the shop. In that moment, she'd known everything was going to be all right. She hadn't realized how frightened she was until the relief hit her at the sight of her big, strong husband appearing with fire in his eyes.

Jack's words had stayed with her. Maybe he'd said everything Seagal never had, or never could. Perhaps he'd merely been trying to help his partner out by tossing some guy talk over the troubled waters.

She intended to find out. It mattered so much to her, and as Mathilda had said, what she and Seagal did would matter greatly to the babies.

The babies wanted to eat, so she fed them and put them to bed. She sat down to calm her nerves, telling herself that Christmas was a time to be happy. To be thankful.

She was thankful for Seagal.

She loved Seagal. She'd fallen in love with him before she'd ever asked him out. She owed it to her children to find out if she and their father could make their marriage work.

Seagal came in the door at eight o'clock, looking weary—but carrying a huge bouquet of white lilies and red roses. "There's only one flower shop in town, so I stopped by and picked these up for you."

She smiled and took the flowers. "Thank you."

He tossed his hat on the flowered sofa. "I sort of worried that it's not acceptable to give your wife flowers from her own shop. Kind of takes the luster off the gesture, you know?"

"It's fine." She sat down on the sofa. "You probably want a shower and a glass of wine? A beer?"

He nodded. "You're going to want me to tell you everything."

"Yes, I am." Capri nodded. "I have a funny feeling that there's a lot I didn't want to accept. And that I haven't been very nice to you about it."

"Shower first," Seagal said. "Then I'll fill in the story for you."

"You know where the shower is."

He nodded, gauging her underlying message. "I'll be right back."

She watched him leave, took a deep breath. It was late, and she knew Seagal had to be hungry. The flowers he'd brought her were beautiful; she thought maybe they were the most wonderful gift he'd ever given her. He'd been trying to be thoughtful—romantic, perhaps—even as his case was winding down.

The tree twinkled softly, another gift from him. And the babies.

He'd changed. She'd changed.

She hoped they'd changed, and that their marriage might be stronger for the changes.

Capri went to the kitchen and put out a plate for herself and her husband, making sure the turkey and the oyster stuffing were still warm. Two crystal wineglasses went beside the plates; she filled them with white wine. Mrs. Penny had put cranberry sauce in the fridge, as well as an apple pie and sides of broccoli and mashed potatoes. These she warmed, and put it all on the table along with a crusty half loaf of French bread.

Seagal came out of the bathroom, his hair damp and tousled. "That looks good."

"Mrs. Penny is a dear friend. She said she made double so we would have a meal and some leftovers."

"She's good, no question. Jack is a lucky nephew." He pulled out her chair. "Are you going to join me?"

"Sure." She took the seat he offered, her heart beating fast.

"Sara and Carter are dreaming of sugarplums?"

"Probably for another sixty seconds."

Seagal smiled. "We better eat fast."

Capri wondered how many meals they'd had at this kitchen table in the two years they'd been married. Had Seagal ever cut the turkey and filled her plate, as he was doing now?

"You don't have to do everything, Seagal," she said. "You weren't the reason our marriage wasn't working. We had equal shares in that."

"When you've had something then lost it, you probably want to work a little harder to keep it if you get another chance." He handed her the plate, began to fill his.

She held her breath. It was too close, too soon. She didn't want him feeling as if he had to work hard to "keep" her; she had just as much work to do. The time he'd spent at his job had been as much an issue for her. Time apart had made her hope that their marriage might be stronger.

"Thank you for today," she said softly.

He shrugged. "It's my job."

They began to eat. Capri found herself listening for the babies, but there wasn't a sound from the nursery. Maybe she had time to say the things she wanted to say more than anything. "You've done so much for me, Seagal. I really appreciate it."

"You're my wife. Those are my children sleeping down the hall. Of course I'm going to take care of you." He sighed as he bit into Mrs. Penny's mashed potatoes. "She may be a gossip, but she's also a heck of a cook."

Capri smiled. "Do you miss Bridesmaids Creek?"

He sipped his wine. "There are things about Bridesmaids Creek I miss."

"I would never want to live anywhere else. I often felt as if you were smothered by this place."

"No. I always knew I'd come home to Bridesmaids Creek. But I had a job to do, and I did it."

The turkey was moist and delicious; the cranberry sauce delicately sweet. Their Christmas Eve meal was so different from last year's. Seagal felt so far away from her. She couldn't eat any more; her stomach was tied in knots. "I'm going to check on the babies."

She left the kitchen, went down the hall to quietly open the nursery door. They had a baby monitor in the kitchen and in the bedroom; still, she felt that she needed to look at them to make certain they were all right.

"Are they ready for *The Night Before Christmas?*" Seagal asked from behind her. He looked over her shoulder at the babies. "Maybe tomorrow night."

She closed the door, following him back to the kitchen. "Apple pie? Mrs. Penny's specialty."

"I think I'd like a fire in the fireplace. You feeling like a fire?"

Capri nodded. "I'll get the wineglasses."

They went into the formal room where the Christmas tree gently glowed. Seagal made a fire, and Capri watched from the flowered sofa.

"Seagal?"

He turned his head. "Yes?"

"Is your assignment over?"

He turned back to the fire. "Capri, my assignment was to play Santa for the kiddies."

"An assignment Mrs. Penny is eager for you to reprise next year."

"She mentioned it. I've accepted."

She was a bit surprised. "Well, you did do justice to the revered Santa suit. I just didn't think you'd want to."

"You'll be cochairing Christmastown, won't you?"

She nodded. "And the Bridesmaids Creek annual swim, and the Groomsmen's Dash. Wherever I'm needed."

"It's time I take on a few things myself. Wearing a Santa cap won't kill me."

She thought about the "bad" boys who'd apparently decided BC needed to add some drug-dealing to their peaceful streets. "What about Kinsler and his gang of nasties? What happens to them now?"

"Actually, we don't know if Taylor Kinsler or any of his ilk were behind the drugs. I talked to Daisy. She claims not to know a single thing about what was going on. I believe her."

A sharp arrow darted into Capri's heart. Bridesmaids Creek was a small town; he would always run into Daisy. So would she. She had to make peace with that. “If she wasn’t being forthright, you would know, Seagal. You’re a good Ranger.”

He looked bemused by her praise. Surprised.

“Have you forgiven me for staking out your store? I’m sorry I couldn’t tell you everything about the case, which I know came across as ham-handed and overbearing. I had to risk your trust in order to protect you.”

“I know now. It was just so hard for me to accept that the world I’d built might be hiding something so horrible for Bridesmaids Creek. It wasn’t until that creep came through the back door and grabbed me that I realized I’d underestimated your cop skills.”

He stood, surveying the fire he’d built. “I’m sorry that happened. I mistook the timing of the next pickup.”

“So is it over?”

“I doubt your store will be used again for the same purpose. They’ll move elsewhere.”

“Somewhere else in Bridesmaids Creek? What about other business owners?”

“I’m going to take an assignment here for a while. I want to be with the babies. Help you out.”

She didn’t say anything, hearing a new tone creep into his voice. Something distant, something cool. “It’s important for you to be with the children, Seagal. I know I didn’t tell you immediately—”

“Your brother took care of me.”

“I’ll talk to Beau about that one day. Anyway, Seagal, I apologize. I really do.” She looked at Seagal. “You’re a wonderful father. I want you to spend all the time with them you can.”

She felt tears gather in her eyes. He looked at her for a long moment, then nodded. “I’m going out for a bit.”

Her breath left her. “Thank you for the flowers.”

He nodded. "Merry Christmas, Capri." He handed her the key to the house.

Then he left.

SEAGAL HATED TO LEAVE Capri, but there was something he had to do.

He had wanted nothing more than to protect her, but he'd come to realize he couldn't. The moment he saw her go inside her shop, Seagal knew that he *had* been overbearing, overprotective. There was no way to keep anybody in a box, keep them safe, the way he wanted to keep Capri safe. She'd had every right to be annoyed with him.

The thing was, he was always going to want to protect her. He just couldn't. She didn't want him to.

But he could take care of his children. He'd always have that part of their marriage. Even after tomorrow, when morning dawned on the day after Christmas, he would know that Carter and Sara would always be a part of both of them.

He found Taylor Kinsler in the Wedding Diner, eating with his gang of "Bad." Seagal pulled up a chair, spoiling for trouble. It was Christmas Eve, and there was no better time to start ringing in the holiday.

"Hello, fellows," Seagal said.

The five men stared him down. He'd gone to school with them, played football with them, even occasionally rodeoed against them. Then their paths had diverged. He'd gone on to become a cop, something that was as much a part of him as breathing. Moving up to the Rangers brought him pride he could hardly explain.

"Don't you have someplace to be on Christmas Eve?" Taylor asked. "Or did the little lady kick you out?"

"I did have plans for Christmas Eve." He leaned back

in the chair. "Unfortunately, I had to participate in a small incident at the Bridesmaids Bouquet flower shop. My wife owns that store," Seagal said, "in case you didn't know. It means a whole lot to her."

The five Bads watched him carefully.

"We found marijuana seeds in some planters from her shop," Seagal said in a conversational tone, "which I was surprised to find in a small town. Funny that anyone would think a flower shop is the perfect place to conceal drugs."

"Why are you telling us?" Taylor asked. "Do we look like we care about drugs? We're sitting here eating burgers and trying to get some holiday spirit, which is kind of hard to do with a cop in our midst."

"Just letting you know I'm going to be in town for a long time." Seagal smiled. "In case you hear anything."

"We don't know anybody who uses drugs," one of the Bad said. "Can't help you."

"I don't need help," Seagal said. "I'm trying to help you." He got up, stared down at the five men. "It was small-time stuff, really. A small-time criminal was sent to make the pickup, too. He squealed like a pig when we pressed him on who'd hired him." Seagal put some money on the table. "I'll buy your meal, fellows. Because I have a funny feeling it's the last one you're going to be eating on the outside for quite some time."

He left, feeling pretty good about everything. It had all worked out.

Everything except his marriage.

That was the one thing he still needed to fix.

Chapter Ten

Capri thought long and hard before she sent the text to Seagal.

The babies have put cookies out for Santa. The key is under the mat.

She sent it, feeling nervous. But Seagal had seemed so strange when he left. She knew something had been on his mind. Cop stuff was always on his mind.

But she knew she was on his mind, too. Capri knelt beside the tree, rearranged some of the gifts people had brought for the babies and for her and Seagal. The stockings were full of tiny baby socks and rattles, and well wishes from friends. Her mother had come by with a carload of gifts—and a letter from her grandmother written to Capri when she was a child, and saved by her mother for the right time.

Dear Capri,

What a wonderful granddaughter you are! So headstrong and stubborn—these are gifts—and beautiful and wise. You remind me so much of myself at your age. I love that you come on Saturdays and work in the shop. I hope you'll always want to spend time with me, because you mean so much to me. I never dreamed I'd have such a considerate granddaughter, and it makes me so happy to see how much you and your mother love each other. We are strong women, we Snows, and I know you will grow up to be a fine woman and mother in your own right one day. I always dreamed I'd have a little granddaughter to make Christmas dresses for. I'm the happiest grandmother in the world. I love you so much, dear sweet granddaughter.

Nana

Capri put the letter away, glanced at the photo of her grandmother on the mantel. "You would have loved your great-grandchildren," she told the photo. "Seagal and I have the most amazing angels."

She turned back to the tree, resettled the gifts, rearranged some bows. She'd hidden a small gift for Seagal under the tree, wrapped in silver and gold with a red bow.

She didn't know if he'd come home to get it.

Her heart would break if he didn't.

At the stroke of midnight, she heard the key turn in the lock. Hope rose inside her.

Seagal stepped inside the house, Santa hat perched jauntily atop his dark hair. "Ho, ho, ho! Merry Christmas," he said.

Capri smiled. "Hi, Santa."

Seagal closed the door behind him as cold air from outside blew in along the floor. "It's freezing outside. I got a text about cookies for Santa?"

Capri got up. "Gingerbread men brought by, fresh

from Mrs. Penny's oven. She said she knew of a Ranger who loved cookies and hot tea."

He looked at her, tossed his Santa hat on the flowered sofa. "I don't know if I can eat the cookies the babies put out for Santa Claus."

Capri looked at her husband. "How about cookies your wife puts out for you?"

He remained by the door, not stepping a foot closer to her. "After tomorrow, I don't think I'll have a wife."

"Something tells me I'm going to have a husband. I think the Christmas spirit has made me believe the thing I want most will be here for Christmas."

A smile bloomed on Seagal's face. "You want a husband more than anything?"

"No," Capri said, moving within arm's length of Seagal, "not just a husband. I want you, Seagal."

He studied her for a moment, glanced around the room, took in the Christmas tree. His gaze settled back on her again. "I'm overbearing and protective."

She nodded. "Yes, you are. And not much for sharing your feelings."

"And that's okay?"

Capri smiled. "Yes to the first two—we'll work on the last one." She put her hand in his. "You're also a fine man. A loving father. And the man I'm in love with."

He drew her into his arms. "Whatever made you change your mind, I'm thankful for. I want you to be happy, even if it means walking into the courthouse tomorrow."

She leaned up to kiss him. He stayed very still, accepting her caress. "How about we just stay in bed? And play with the babies when they wake up?"

His eyes lit with everything she'd ever wanted to know about his feelings: love, desire, happiness. "I love you," Seagal said. "I love my children, because you gave them to me." He kissed her thoroughly, making sure she had no doubt of the way he felt about her. He pulled back, looked into her eyes. "Come on, Mrs. Claus. Let's go look at our little sugarplums."

They walked down the hall hand in hand, stopping outside the nursery. Seagal pushed open the door, and they went to stand by the babies' cribs. Carter and Sara lay under their soft blankets, their tiny eyelids closed tightly with not a care in the world.

"Nestled all snug in their beds," Seagal said. "They don't even know it's Christmas."

"I do," Capri said. "And I have something to give you. Something that requires you to do a little unwrapping."

Capri smiled as Seagal picked her up in his arms. She put her head on his chest, loving being back in his strong arms again. He carried her from the nursery, and as they went through the kitchen, Capri snagged the plate of cookies she'd laid out for Santa.

After all, Santa needed to keep his strength up. She fully intended that her husband would have a very merry Christmas—every year for the rest of their lives.

Epilogue

The babies slept in for the first time ever on Christmas morning, but as soon as their little cries came over the baby monitor, Seagal and Capri unwrapped themselves from each other's arms and dressed.

They hurried down the hall into the nursery. Seagal picked up Sara, and Capri took Carter from his crib.

"Good morning, beautiful," Seagal said. "Merry Christmas, babies," he said, snuggling his daughter's cheek. Sara stopped crying, taking in her father's deep voice and touch. Seagal grinned at Capri. "Santa said thank you very much for the delicious cookies you put out for him, babies."

"Yes," Capri said, changing Carter's diaper. "We're all very grateful about that."

Seagal looked at his wife. "Grateful?"

She laughed. "Aren't you?"

"I was thinking that I was more blown away, knocked to my knees and charmed."

She smiled, swapping him Carter for Sara. "All that over cookies?"

He handed Carter back to his mother. "I can change my daughter's diaper," he said, "and yes, that's exactly how I feel about my wife."

He finished the diaper and picked his daughter

up, making room for Carter in his arms, too. "I think they're ready for their Christmas breakfast."

Capri fed the babies by the Christmas tree, enjoying the warm glow of the tree and the fire Seagal made in the fireplace. Then they put the babies on a blanket in front of the tree, and sat next to them.

"It's a lot of gifts for two tiny people," Seagal said, looking at all the gaily wrapped boxes.

"And something for you," Capri said, handing him a present.

He looked at his wife as she sat in her red satin bathrobe. Her eyes were shining with happiness—she was the most beautiful woman he'd ever seen. "You already gave me these tiny bundles of joy," he said. "And you." He kissed her, giving her a taste of later, when he intended to kiss her thoroughly again. "Quite frankly, your text about the cookies and house key pretty much made my night."

"This is just a little something extra," Capri said.

He opened the box, pulling out a framed black-and-white photo of Capri and the babies sitting in front of the Christmas tree. He grinned. "How'd you know this is exactly what I wanted?"

Capri smiled. "The babies told me."

"They're pretty discerning children." He took her hands in his, kissing her fingertips. "Capri, I never dreamed you would give me another chance. I know I haven't been much for telling you how I feel, but I won't forget in the future. I always thought you knew how I felt about you, but—" He kissed her fingertips again, then put them over his heart. "I know a marriage is stronger when the feelings are shared."

She smiled. "I think so, too."

He took a deep breath. "But I'm hoping for one more Christmas miracle."

She looked at him, her gaze questioning.

"Our marriage is the most important thing in the world to me," Seagal said. "Is there any chance you'd want to renew our vows? As you said before, we got married pretty fast. I'm not sure if you feel it was too rushed. As much as I was never one for talking much, I think saying our vows again would be a wonderful way for us to start off our new lives together."

Seagal thought his wife practically glowed with happiness. Capri moved close to him, and he pulled her onto his lap. "I'd love that," she said. "Thank you for thinking of it."

"I'm trying out this new more romantic persona," Seagal said.

"And I'm impressed," Capri said, kissing him.

"You're going to sidetrack me," Seagal said, enjoying his wife's lips. "And you don't want to sidetrack me before I give you your present."

She looked at him. "I feel like you've given me so much, Seagal, not the least of which what you did for my flower shop. I can't think what would have happened to my grandmother's store if you hadn't been so vigilant. I'm pretty sure I would have lost the business," Capri said. "I can't imagine it getting shut down by the DEA or whatever. All my grandmother's hard work lost."

"Best to stamp it out while it was a small op," Seagal said. "Although I have no doubt that the Bads will figure out a new game. I'll be keeping a close eye on them in the future."

"Still, between my store and these beautiful babies, I feel like you've given me everything." She leaned against his chest.

"Now that we've established me as a bona fide Santa Stud," Seagal said, "let's see how this fits."

He handed her a tiny box wrapped in silver with a gold bow on top, so small she hadn't even seen it resting on one of the branches. "When did you do this?"

"After the bust." He looked at his sleeping babies, then kissed his wife. "I guess I got so nervous when I realized you'd been in danger that I panicked. Apparently when I panic, I go shopping for my wife."

"Oh, Seagal," she said, opening the box. "It's so beautiful!"

He smiled as she gingerly picked up the gold-and-diamond wedding band. "Merry Christmas, babe."

She gazed at him. "It's a pretty spectacular present, Santa."

Taking the band from her, Seagal slid it onto her finger behind the diamond engagement ring he'd noticed she'd never taken off. "Well, Mrs. West, it occurred to me that a man gives his wife a wedding ring when he's planning to marry her. If I ever forget to say the words, I hope you'll know how much I love you when you look at this ring. Because I do love you. I always did. I will forever."

"That's the Christmas present I wanted," she whispered, and he kissed her, savoring the magic of holding his wife in his arms again. He smiled at his babies sleeping peacefully on the blanket, and the fire in the fireplace and the twinkling Christmas tree—and even the flowered sofa that somehow he'd grown to appreciate.

It was a magical Christmas, the best he'd ever had. Because Christmas was in the heart, and his heart was with his family—where it had longed to be.

* * * * *

The Christmas Rescue

REBECCA WINTERS

Dear Reader,

We've all heard the expression "When God closes a door, He always opens a window." It's a great saying. I've pondered it many times in regard to those things affecting my life as well as the lives of others. In this Christmas story, I decided to take two negatives and turn them into a positive.

Christmas is supposed to be a time of happiness and joy when the world celebrates the birth of Christ. Yet what could be more negative than for a woman to be fleeing a terrifying situation at this time of year? And what about a man who would like to blot out Christmas from his consciousness after the pain another Christmas brought him?

These people meet under the most unlikely circumstances involving a precious baby. You'll have to read the story to find out that miracles *do* happen, even at the most improbable moment to two people who had a door close on them and definitely need a window opened.

Enjoy!

Rebecca Winters

I'd like to dedicate this book to all law enforcement workers, firefighters, paramedics and hospital workers everywhere. These heroes and heroines sacrifice their lives and time year round, but especially during the holidays, in order to serve the rest of us.

Chapter One

Have yourself a very Merry Christmas.

The cheery holiday song serenaded Andrea Sinclair as she entered the car dealership, but it did nothing to ease her fear and anxiety. She was in a great hurry.

"Pick out any model you want off the floor, and I'll wrap it up for you to drive home in half an hour tops!"

At the sound of the salesman's voice, Andrea jerked around, clutching her three-month-old son tighter. "Are you George?"

"Oh—you've talked to him already?" He was clearly disappointed.

"Yes. On the phone earlier. Could you let him know I'm here to get the Honda?"

"Sure." He walked away. In another minute she heard George being paged. "You have a customer waiting out in front."

Seconds later, a young man came bounding across the showroom floor. "You're Andrea?"

"Yes."

"Good. I've got your Honda washed and ready to go. Where's your Sentra?"

"In the bay where they did the inspection. I left the title on the seat."

"Perfect. I'll drive it around to the used-car lot. Just

walk past these offices to the back and I'll meet you out there."

She handed him her car keys. "Thank you so much. You have no idea how grateful I am." Her voice shook despite her best effort to remain calm in front of him.

"Hey—I made some money. It all helps this close to Christmas."

Christmas.

Andrea couldn't think of the holidays now. For three months she'd been living in fear of her husband. Escape was the only thing on her mind.

She kissed Jack's cheek. "Come on, sweetheart. We're going for a ride." *Let's pray we get a long way past the border before our junker car conks out.*

Outside, she saw to her relief George had parked her two-year-old car next to the nine-year-old green one she'd just purchased. That made it easier for her to transfer the car seat and her suitcase. The last thing to grab was the diaper bag.

She noticed the rear windshield where the temporary permit had been stuck on; her license plates would come later. George motioned to her from the glassed-in office. While her baby son kept turning his head to look at everything, she signed the papers and in a few minutes was ready to go.

"Good luck, Mrs. Sinclair. Merry Christmas." He handed her the keys along with the dealership's calendar for the New Year.

"Merry Christmas to you, too. Thank you for everything."

In a rush, Andrea got Jack settled and strapped in to his car seat. After giving him another kiss and a plastic doughnut toy to bite on, she got in the front seat and started the engine. She was relieved when the car hummed smoothly to life. George had even filled the tank with gas. *I owe him.*

The huge dealership sprawled across several lot lengths. She wound around to a place where nobody would notice her and pulled out the jaw-length brown wig she'd bought. Andrea pinned her pale blond ponytail on top of her head, then pulled on the wig. The change was so remarkable, even she didn't recognize herself.

Jack would probably start crying when he didn't recognize her, but she didn't have time to worry about that right now. She looked around, buckled up and then took off. After a few minutes she reached the 285 leading south out of Carlsbad, New Mexico, and headed for Texas.

She'd tossed her old cell phone and had bought a new one that couldn't be traced. No one could reach her now except her attorney, Sheila North. The older woman had warned her to tell no one her new number, not even her best friends. Andrea had been following her advice to the letter.

Thanks to her, Andrea had a safe place to go. She glanced at the map she'd marked. Alpine, Texas, was her destination. If there were no problems with the car, she ought to be there by evening. It was only a three-hour drive. Though the sky looked grizzly and threatened rain, the bad weather didn't bother her. She and Jack were finally leaving.

She had a premonition Jerry would try to break in to her apartment tonight. He'd been harassing her with phone calls and emails, telling her no restraining order could stop him from talking to her. But she wouldn't be there. Not ever again. He'd violated his supervised visitation rights for the last time.

When he couldn't find her car, he wouldn't have any idea where she'd gone. She wouldn't put it past him to threaten her friends if they didn't break their silence, but it wouldn't do him any good. Her friends knew nothing and Andrea had left no clues.

Twice en route she pulled into a rest area, once to change Jack and another time to feed him. Each time, she removed the wig while she took care of him. Her little darling was being so good.

Replacing her disguise, she got going. Now a heavy rain was coming down. After a few miles she saw the big sign she'd been waiting for at the side of the road. A cry of relief escaped her lips. Welcome to Texas. Drive Friendly—Texas Way.

"It won't be long now, Jack." She consulted her map. When they came to Fort Davis, she'd buy dinner and gas up. Alpine wouldn't be that much farther away. For a distraction, she turned on the radio and listened to the news. The weather forecast was predicting snow in the Davis Mountains. The newscaster said it was a rare occurrence and warned people in that area to be prepared.

Andrea switched off the radio. So far there was only rain, but she was anxious to reach the next town just in case she ran into a blizzard. She'd stop at a drive-through for a hamburger and then feed Jack. If the weather got really bad, she'd find a motel for the night and drive on to Alpine tomorrow. Anxious as she was to put distance between her and Jerry, her first priority was her darling son, whose routine had been disrupted enough.

The sky had grown dark as pitch, which might explain why there was little traffic going in either direction. She was slogging through a slushy downpour when suddenly snow started in earnest. Soon she came to the outskirts of Fort Davis; Alpine was only twenty more miles.

Debating whether to stay here or go on, she spotted a convenience center at the next corner and pulled in next to the nearest pump. No matter what, she needed gas. A camper van pulled up to one of the other pumps.

"I'll be right back, Jack." Reaching for her credit card, she jumped out into the snow. The temperature had taken a plunge; at this point, a motel sounded good. Anxious to finish her task and find lodging for the night, she'd swiped the card and started to release the gas nozzle when she was suddenly knocked from behind and thrown forward into the snow.

FLYNN PATTERSON DROVE his truck along 118 headed for Fort Davis. The violence of the elements matched his mood and kept sensible people off the roads. Visibility was bad, and he pulled over to the side of the road to adjust his windshield wipers so he could see. The snow hit him like an arctic blast, but he relished it. Anything to drive out the pain.

Three days, and Christmas would be here. If he could just burrow into this freezing wilderness and not think until it was all over, he might survive to live again for another year.

For what?

If his psychiatrist heard him ask that question again, he'd tell him he needed to check in to the hospital for some intense therapy. His siblings would fall apart if they knew his state of mind.

What do you mean if *they knew, Patterson?*

No one talked about the Christmas season around him, not his family, not his friends or colleagues. The time of holiday cheer represented a loss to him too terrible to revisit. He was thankful that his married sisters lived in Houston and knew enough to leave him alone.

While he drove, he could hear the chatter of the dispatcher taking calls at police headquarters. It kept him distracted. Flynn had just solved a big murder case near Van Horn and was officially off duty. He had one choice at this point. Go home and get reacquainted with the three-quarter-full bottle of Jack Daniel's in the cupboard.

It would take the entire contents to blot out the pictures of his wife and daughter, killed on a commuter flight from Dallas to Houston two years ago.

It had been only three days before Christmas....

Pain welled from his gut, filling his eyes with tears. As he was attempting to choke them down, he saw something on his left that jerked him back to his surroundings. Snow had been falling steadily, but he'd noticed that a set of car tracks coming from the opposite direction had suddenly disappeared over an embankment.

He did a quick U-turn and drove to the place where the tracks went off the road. They were almost buried now, but whoever had lost control of the car had to have done so in the past five minutes. He called Fort Davis for backup and gave the coordinates, then he turned off his engine.

Pulling on his gloves, he grabbed his flashlight and stepped sideways down the deep culvert. An older-model green Honda had rolled several times and landed on its roof.

Before he could reach the accident site, Flynn heard a baby screaming its lungs out. The cries came close to sending his heart into cardiac arrest. He flashed the light around. Glass was everywhere. The front passenger door had come off. Items from the car were scattered in the snow.

He made his way to the open rear window and saw the baby upside down in its car seat. On instinct, he reached to feel the seat belt and undo it, allowing the baby to fall into his arms. Flynn clutched the terrified infant to his chest and raced up the embankment to his truck.

Whipping off his winter parka, he wrapped the little boy in it—at least he assumed it was a boy by the blue jeans and baseball shirt he was wearing. Then he turned on the heat full blast while he examined him. By some miracle he didn't see any blood, but hypothermia could have set in.

The baby was in hysterics, haunting Flynn. "Don't die on me, little guy. Please don't die." He picked him back up and cuddled him against his shoulder, talking to him the way he used to talk to his precious Katie to comfort her.

"There's probably a mother down there unconscious or worse," he told police dispatch. "I haven't heard any other sounds, but the hell of it is, I can't go check while the baby's clinging to me. He's been traumatized by what's happened."

"Understood."

"Where's the damn backup?"

"They should be there any minute, Captain Patterson. Hold on."

Flynn had never been so torn in his life. If that were his wife down there, and no one was helping her… He had to find out.

Hardening himself to the baby's cries, he laid him down on his side on the front passenger seat. The vehicle's interior was nice and warm. "I'll only be gone a minute, buddy. I promise."

Leaving the baby still wailing, he grabbed his gloves and took off down the embankment again. The ghastly scene tore at his gut while he hurried around to the other side of the car. The driver's door had flown open and he saw the body of a man dressed in jeans and a T-shirt. He'd been flung several yards away and lay facedown in the snow. *Another driver who hadn't fastened his seat belt.* Flynn saw no signs of anyone else.

He hunkered down to feel the pulse in the man's neck. He was alive and breathing, but without help, he wouldn't last long. In case he'd broken something, Flynn didn't dare move him. *Please, God.* Get that ambulance here. The baby needed his father. Heaven knew he needed his son.

The faint sounds of the baby's cries galvanized him into action. He spotted a diaper bag farther afield and stole over to reach inside. Sure enough, there was a bottle of ready-mix formula and a baby blanket. Leaving the rest of the accident scene untouched, he grabbed both and hurried back up to the truck.

He brushed the snow off himself and climbed in the cab. "Here I am. I've got something good for you." He opened the bottle and turned the nipple around. "Come on." Flynn gathered the baby in his arms and put the nipple to his mouth.

At first the baby fought him. He was a strong little thing, probably about three months old. Flynn kept at it, coaxing him until he finally gave a huge trembling sigh and started drinking the cold formula. Every so often he'd stop swallowing and cry. "I know how you feel, but you're okay now. Come on. Be a good boy and drink some more for me."

After several urgings, the baby began to relax against him, bringing back memories of comforting his six-month-old girl when she'd bumped into a chair or pinched her little fingers by accident while learning to crawl. It had taken time for her to get over her frights, too.

Babies were a miracle, so fragile in some ways, so strong in others. The poor little guy had been hanging there upside down, but somehow he'd survived.

He heard a knock on the window and let out a hallelujah.

"Everything all right in here?"

"Yes, but the driver down there is barely hanging on."

"We're already bringing him up. Why don't you hand me the baby and I'll take a look at him in the ambulance."

"That's all right. I'll carry him over." One more upset could bring on another fit of hysterics. Flynn got out of the truck, shielding the baby, who'd drained his bottle. Except for an occasional shudder, he seemed more at peace.

By now the police had arrived and were going over the accident scene. When everyone was ready to head into town, Flynn reluctantly handed the baby to the paramedic. That was a mistake. He started crying again. "You go on, Captain. We'll take good care of him."

Flynn had to steel himself to turn his back on the boy. He followed the ambulance through the snow to the hospital E.R. in Fort Davis, not able to get there fast enough. The second he shut off the engine, he shot out of his truck and hurried inside with the officers and paramedics. One of them took the baby to the nursery.

Flynn wanted to go, too, but he couldn't. He was the first responder and had to make a report.

The accident victim's eyes were closed. Flynn could see the poor father had a goose egg on his temple and cuts on his hands and arms, but the paramedics had already started an IV and it appeared he would make it. The two of them had cheated death. His wife would have reason to celebrate this Christmas.

Flynn saw Sheriff Bates, who signaled him over to the desk. "Have you heard the latest?"

"What?"

"A woman was found slumped in the snow outside a pump at Barton's Convenience Mart on Pine Street earlier this evening named Andrea Sinclair. A motorist saw her and called 911. When they brought her in, she was screaming in terror that her husband had stolen her baby. She was afraid she'd never see him again."

Husband? This was a domestic-violence dispute? Flynn threw his head back in frustration. The number one rule in this business. Never assume anything.

"As usual, it took one of our Texas Rangers to bring about a miracle this fast." The sheriff kept talking. "Heard you solved the case up in Van Horn. Congratulations. You do great work, Flynn."

"I happened to be passing at the right moment." The older man's remarks were gratifying, but Flynn's mind was on the tragedy of the situation. "I assumed he was the father."

"It's a shame these things happen, and especially around the holidays. The cell phone found in the snow has water damage and isn't working. We presume it's his, since the woman's purse, also lying by the pump, had a cell phone. Except for two hundred dollars cash in his back pocket, he had no ID on him."

"That figures," Flynn muttered in quiet rage. When parents kidnapped their own children, they never thought about the trauma they caused.

"The dispatcher said he was glad he hadn't been in your shoes. He could hear the hysterics."

"It tore me up. I pray he's not going to suffer any residual problems."

"I doubt it. You and I know babies are tough."

Flynn nodded. He'd seen proof of it tonight. The scene was one he'd never forget. "What else do you know so far?"

"Her ID indicates she's from Carlsbad, New Mexico. She's twenty-seven. The car is registered there, too. It was bought today from the Haney dealership. One of the officers found a calendar from there in the snow."

His brows lifted. "Her flight came to a quick end. I need to talk to her." The woman could be on the level. Then again, she might be involved in something ugly—like kidnapping someone else's baby—and everything had gone wrong.

"Go ahead, but she was hysterical and the doctor had to sedate her. When she was attacked, the wind was knocked out of her, but there were no injuries. She was wearing a wig. The officers assume it was a disguise—not because of chemo treatments. After the baby is checked out in the nursery, he'll be reunited with his mom. That ought to bring her out of her shock enough to tell you what happened."

He patted Flynn's shoulder. "Crossing state lines means you've got a kidnapping case to solve. I talked to Nyall. Your boss is sorry about spoiling your Christmas vacation."

Flynn didn't mind. "After I check in with him, I'll

go look in on her and see if she's ready to answer any questions." He now had another choice besides getting blotto on Jack Daniel's. At least for tonight.

Chapter Two

Andrea moved her head back and forth as she became more aware of her surroundings. She'd lost all track of time and could hear people speaking in quiet voices. That excruciating pain was back since the drug they'd given her had worn off. She started to sob. "My baby—has anyone found my baby?"

"We have, Mrs. Sinclair."

She didn't recognize the deep male voice, but those words filled her whole being with unspeakable joy. "Is he all right?"

"He's right here safe and sound. See for yourself."

Andrea felt the hospital bed being raised. The next sight she saw was an unfamiliar man holding her baby, whom he'd just picked up from the hospital crib. Jack was wrapped in one of the blankets she'd packed in the diaper bag. The stranger handed her the bundle with infinite care.

"Oh, my baby—" She clutched Jack to her, trying to hold back the sobs so she wouldn't frighten him. "My little sweetheart." She pressed kisses to his face and hands. "I can't believe I've got you back." She cuddled him close, rocking him.

Jack found his favorite place against her neck and burrowed in. While she smoothed one hand over his little back, she looked up into a pair of the most beautiful, warm gray eyes she'd ever seen. Through his black lashes they looked suspiciously bright as the tall, hard-muscled male with dark sable hair stared down at the two of them. "He's missed his mommy."

"Who are you?" she whispered.

"My name's Flynn Patterson. I'm with the Texas Rangers."

She'd heard of the Rangers all her life. This one wore a Western-style shirt and cowboy boots. If anyone fitted the description of one of those legendary heroes, he did.

"I was the one who happened to come across a car accident earlier tonight outside Fort Davis and discovered your baby locked in his car seat. It's a good thing, too. He survived the rollover without a scratch. All he wanted was you."

Tears flowed down her cheeks. "Thank God you found him—" she cried emotionally. But in the next breath, fear seized her. "What about my husband? I-Is he in the hospital, too?" Her question came out jerkily.

"Yes. The doctor says he's suffered a concussion, but he's going to make it."

She felt the blood drain from her face. "I don't want to see him. Please don't let him come near me or the baby. I filed for divorce five months ago and we've been legally separated since then. But he's been out of control and has continually ignored the restraining orders against him."

"Have no fear. He's under guard on another floor. While Jack is resting comfortably against you, are you up to answering a few questions for me? I need your answers for the record."

"Now that you've found my baby, I'm up for anything! Go ahead."

Andrea watched him snag a chair from the side of the room with effortless male grace and sit down next to the bed with his long powerful legs extended. His wavy hair framed a face with rugged features.

She found him attractive in an unconventional sense. There was an aura of authority about him that made her feel she could trust him. When he caught her staring at him, heat filled her cheeks and she kissed Jack's head to cover her embarrassment.

"What's your husband's name?"

"Jerold Sinclair, but everyone calls him Jerry."

"What does he do for a living?"

"He's a pilot for Western Skies Airlines."

"How old is he?"

"Thirty-four."

"Does he have family?"

"Yes. His parents and brother live in California, but he's estranged from them."

"Let me have their names and addresses."

"All I know is he was raised in Fullerton. I don't have any other details."

"I can check that out. Are you employed?"

"Not right now."

He sat forward. "All right. Now tell me what led up to his kidnapping your baby. Try to remember as much as you can so you don't have to go through this again. I'm recording our conversation through a mini device hooked to my pocket."

If he hadn't told her that, she wouldn't have had any idea. "A year and a half ago, I met Jerry while I was working in the programming department of a local television station in Carlsbad."

"Which one?"

Andrea told him and gave him the name of her former boss. "I'd been there since graduating from college five years ago. Jerry and I got married three months after meeting each other, and last January I found out I was expecting."

She shifted Jack to her other shoulder. "I worked up until the last three months of my pregnancy, when the doctor put me on bed rest. Jerry didn't handle that well. He wanted a wife who could play between flights. I hardly saw him.

"One day I received a call from a man who told me Jerry had been involved with a flight attendant in Albuquerque since before our marriage and was still seeing her. He thought I ought to know. I'm sure one of the other pilots who knew what was going on got someone to call. I didn't recognize the voice.

"At first I didn't want to believe it, but lying there in bed I started putting two and two together. It explained a lot of things I hadn't been able to understand. Jerry had taken no interest in getting ready for the baby. And then I bought some things for the baby online, but my credit card was declined for insufficient funds.

"Upon investigation I found out not only was our checking account overdrawn but he'd used up most of the money from my savings account accrued over five years of working. I was so shaken—I realized I didn't know the man I'd trusted so completely.

"When Jerry got home from his latest flight, I confronted him about everything. He admitted he had a gambling problem and was in financial trouble. As for the affair, he didn't deny it, but said it was over and it hadn't meant anything. He made all kinds of promises that he'd recoup the losses and make it all up to me.

"That's when I told him our marriage was over and I had filed for divorce. On the advice of my attorney,

I took the little money left in my savings account and moved to a furnished apartment before the baby was born."

"What's your attorney's name and phone number?"

"Sheila North, with Bradford and Gonzales." Andrea gave him the number. "After the baby came, she arranged visitation through Jerry's attorney. While I've been waiting for the divorce to be final, Jerry has kept coming over when it wasn't his time to see Jack, insisting we needed to talk and get back together.

"His harassment prompted me to get a restraining order and my attorney arranged for supervised visitation. That only enraged him. He made threats over the phone and drove over to my apartment all the time, pounding on the door in the middle of the night. He came so often, I decided he was desperate for money.

"Two days ago I had a long talk with my attorney and she said I needed to disappear. She knew of a safe house for battered women in Alpine, Texas, where I could get help and find a job. I was so frightened of Jerry at that point, I told her I would do it, because I've had no living family to help me since my aunt died.

"In order to fool him, I drove my Sentra to the car dealership yesterday, and traded it in on an older Honda. Then I drove out the back way wearing a wig I'd purchased, and I left the state.

"It was snowing so hard I decided to stay here overnight. I stopped for gas first. While I was dealing with the nozzle, I got shoved from behind and the fall dazed me. The next thing I knew, the car with my baby in it was gone. I realized immediately it was Jerry—" Her body trembled uncontrollably. "He'd warned me he would do something drastic to get my attention."

"But you didn't actually see him?"

"No, I didn't have to. After what he's put me through, I've feared what he'd do, but I didn't think even he would put our baby in jeopardy. Do you imagine he thought I'd give him the little money I had left to pay a ransom to get Jack back? Obviously all my efforts to hide from him have been in vain. A kind stranger happened to see me and called the police. They brought me here. You know the rest."

He eyed her compassionately. "Do you recall seeing anyone else at that convenience mart?"

She hugged her baby tighter. "No. There was no one around. Wait—I do remember that a camper pulled up to get gas at another pump. The storm was so bad by then, there were hardly any cars out."

Something flickered in his eyes. "Do you remember the make or color?"

Andrea bit her lip. "There was too much snow and I really wasn't paying attention. It looked like one of those camper trucks. I'm sure it wasn't new."

"That all helps. I'll alert the police to keep an eye out for it while they're on duty. In the meantime I'll check with the sales person inside the mart and question the stranger who called 911. Maybe one of them will be able to shed more light."

"You think Jerry was driving that camper?" The mere thought sent a river of ice through her veins.

"It's possible. If so, he had an accomplice with him, because there was no sign of the camper when the police arrived to take care of you. What kind of car does your husband normally drive?"

"A two-year-old black Audi."

The Ranger got to his feet. "Where's your cell phone? I'll program my number into it in case you need to phone me."

"It's right here on the bedside table." She handed it to him.

He did it quickly and handed the phone back to her. "Now give me your number." He whipped out his phone and programmed her number. "Thank you for your time, Mrs. Sinclair. I'll leave you alone with your baby and see you tomorrow to finish up my investigation. I trust you and Jack will be able to sleep now. Make it a long one. After your harrowing experience, you both deserve it."

If anyone deserved the same, it was the Ranger. Andrea wanted to call him back, but realized he was probably exhausted so she didn't say anything. He'd told her he'd see her tomorrow. She would make sure of it, because she planned to thank him again for giving her back her baby and her sanity.

ONCE HE'D LEFT Andrea's room, Flynn went up to the second-floor nursing station to check with the doctor who'd been taking care of Jerry Sinclair. "Have you communicated with the man since he was brought in?"

"No. He's been in a dazed condition."

"While in that state, has he called out a name?"

The doctor blinked. "No… Wait, yes—but not a name. He cursed and said something like 'I'm screwed.'"

Interesting.

"Let me know as soon as he's able to talk. I'll be in the lounge at the end of the hall."

No point driving home in the snow. There was nothing to go home to, and he'd have to be back here by eight to interrogate the patient. Flynn had slept in hospital lounges before and could do it again. He'd rather be here anyway if the patient became coherent enough to be questioned sooner than later.

After the doctor nodded, Flynn walked down the hall reflecting on their conversation. The first thing an agonized father who loved his child would have done was call out his child's name or his wife's name, even if he'd been caught in a criminal act. That wasn't this patient's initial instinct. It sent up a red flag.

Mrs. Sinclair had said she hadn't actually seen her husband. There was one way to find out if the man who occupied that hospital bed was indeed Mr. Sinclair. Flynn had a gut feeling he wasn't, otherwise he would have carried ID to prove he was the baby's father and had the right to be with him.

Tomorrow he'd take some pictures of him with his cell phone and ask her to look at them for a positive identification.

Her story wasn't that different from so many domestic-violence cases, except for one thing. Little Jack Sinclair had gotten to Flynn when the baby had finally snuggled against his chest. For the first time in two years, Flynn's arms hadn't felt empty.

What a sight it was to see the little boy nestled against his mommy, so happy and secure. Both were blond and beautiful. When Flynn realized where his thoughts had wandered, he checked his watch. Ten after three.

He could take his pick of the empty couches in the lounge, and he stretched out on the longest one. It was still too short. Before he did anything else, he phoned the number for Sheila North. The menu gave him an emergency number. He pushed the digits and waited.

A woman who'd obviously been asleep answered. "This is Sheila North."

Flynn got right to the point. Within a minute relief washed over him to learn Andrea Sinclair had told him the truth about her case. For some reason that made little sense, he hadn't wanted to suspect her of any wrongdoing.

After promising to keep in touch with the attorney, he hung up and set his watch alarm for eight. But he needn't have bothered, because the doctor wakened him at seven. "Captain Patterson?"

Flynn sat up, instantly alert.

"I'm going off duty, but wanted you to know the patient is awake."

"I appreciate your letting me know. What's his condition?"

"He's recovering from a concussion. Barring complications, he can be released into police custody tomorrow."

"Have you found out his name?"

"He won't talk."

He would when Flynn got through with him. "Thanks for the information."

As the doctor walked away, Flynn got to his feet and found a restroom to freshen up. The mirror told him he looked like hell. He needed a shower and shave, but that would have to wait.

Wanting a pickup, he bought a cola out of the vending machine and phoned headquarters. An officer needed to talk to both the person who'd found Mrs. Sinclair and the person on duty at the convenience mart and get any information they could to help the case. With that accomplished he headed to the patient's room. One of the police officers on duty was seated in a chair outside. The two nodded.

With the door ajar, he could hear the nurse telling the patient to cooperate so she could take his blood pressure. While Flynn waited for her to finish checking the man's vital signs, he pulled out his cell phone and primed it so he could take pictures on the spot.

In another minute the nurse came out of the room looking rattled. He took that moment to slip in. The patient had been hooked up to another IV and was in restraints. His arms were covered in tattoos. Flynn started taking pictures. The patient saw him and turned his head. So much the better. That gave him some side-view angles for his mug photo.

He would email them to Nyall with instructions to put them into the computer's database for a possible match. Flynn moved over to the bed. Going on a hunch, he said, "How much did Jerry Sinclair pay you to do his dirty work for him?" If her husband hadn't been in that camper, then he'd probably hired a couple of guys to shake her up, and the other one was long gone with the camper.

The man turned his head to the other side.

"You're under arrest for kidnapping, stealing personal property and attempting to cross state lines, which is a federal offense. Assaulting Mrs. Sinclair at the gas pump adds another grievous charge to the list. They're stacking up against you. You want to cooperate first by telling me your name?"

"Go to hell. I want an attorney."

"Both can be arranged. I'll be back. While I'm gone, consider that if you tell me all you know about Mrs. Sinclair's husband, I'll get your sentence lightened when the judge throws the book at you."

Chapter Three

One of the police officers had brought all Andrea's possessions gathered at the accident site to the room. While the baby slept, she showered and washed her hair, then changed into another pair of jeans and a blue cotton sweater with long sleeves.

The doctor had done his rounds and declared her and the baby fit enough to leave the hospital, on two conditions. First, he wanted her to check in to a motel and take it easy for another twenty-four hours before she did anything else. Second, she couldn't leave the hospital until Captain Patterson had talked to her again. This was a federal matter and he was in charge of the investigation.

Andrea had no intention of leaving until she saw the Ranger again. She owed him her life, because if he hadn't found Jack, her life wouldn't have been worth living. She needed to tell him that in person.

While she drank the juice from her breakfast tray, she heard a knock on the door.

"Come in."

Her senses quickened as the Ranger who'd been on her mind walked into the room. She decided he'd been up all night, since he had a noticeable beard, but it only made him more appealing, if that was possible.

"Good morning, Mrs. Sinclair."

"It's a wonderful morning because of you," she said in a tremulous voice. Andrea started to get up from the chair, but he told her to remain seated and finish her food. Tears smarted her eyes. "How do I thank you for what you've done?"

"All the thanks I need is right here." He'd walked over to the crib and smiled down at her son. "He's sleeping so soundly, you'd never know he'd lived through such an ordeal." He glanced at her out of eyes shot with silver. "The fact that he's alive is a miracle."

"I know," she whispered. "Your being there at the right time was part of it. I'll never be able to thank you enough."

"It's my job."

She shook her head. "It's a lot more than that. You deal with life and death every day. I'm convinced you were born with the extra capacity to help your fellow man. My baby is very lucky."

His expression sobered as he focused his attention on her. "How are you feeling this morning? I'm talking physically."

"I'm much better than I thought I'd be. The doctor said I could leave the hospital after I talked to you."

"With the caveat that you stay at a motel in town for another day to recover from the shock."

The Ranger knew everything. "Yes, he did say that."

He pulled his cell phone from his pocket. "I'd like you to take a look at some pictures." He walked over to her and leaned down while he slid his thumb across the screen of his iPhone. An awareness of his masculinity caught her off guard. "Do you recognize this man?"

"No. I never saw him in my life."

"He's the criminal who knocked you down and stole your car."

"It wasn't Jerry?" She jerked her head around, but it brought their faces so close, they were almost touching. As she jumped to her feet, he straightened. By now her heart was thudding in her chest for more reasons than one.

"Does this mean it was some thug who decided to steal my car in a random act?" She couldn't believe it.

"My hunch is he and another accomplice are working for your husband."

Andrea felt sick again. "If that's true, then it means Jerry's still out there looking for me."

"Don't worry. I'm going to get you to a safe place."

"Is there such a thing?" A tremor ran through her body. "Jerry has eyes and ears everywhere."

His jaw hardened. "It doesn't matter. If your husband had nothing to do with this, then he doesn't know where you are. Just the same, I'll have my department contact the police in Carlsbad and have him picked up for ignoring the restraining order, and they can question him.

"If it turns out he planned this kidnapping, then he knows it failed and the police are looking for him. He's now a fugitive and I'm going to catch him."

He'd said that with spine-tingling conviction. She shivered when she looked at him. Those gray eyes so warm and tender last night had turned to flint. Jerry would be no match for him. Captain Patterson was a different breed of man.

While she stood there trying to absorb everything, Jack started fussing. She turned to the crib, but the Ranger had gotten there first. "May I?" he asked. "He and I got acquainted last night. I wonder if he'll remember me feeding him a bottle."

She smiled. "I wouldn't be surprised. Go ahead." After what he'd done, Andrea couldn't have denied him if she'd wanted to.

He handled her baby so expertly, he had to be a father himself. "Hey, little guy. How are you this morning?" He put him against his shoulder and walked the floor with him. "I bet you're glad to be back with your mommy."

To her surprise Jack didn't fight being held by him. "I think he *does* remember you."

"Maybe it's my grizzly beard."

She chuckled. "Do you have children?"

He kissed the baby's head. "I did have a daughter. She and my wife, Michelle, were killed in a plane crash two years ago. Katie was only six months old."

"Oh no—" Andrea was devastated by the revelation. There'd been no miracle for him. "It's not fair," she whispered.

"I was thinking the same thing about your situation." He flicked her another glance. "Since you need another place to stay until tomorrow, I'm taking you home with me. It's the best way I know to keep you safe if your husband is in Fort Davis waiting for you to be released from the hospital. After what you've been through emotionally, you and the baby need to get your strength back without any worries."

Andrea was suddenly short of breath. "I couldn't ask you to do that."

"Since your case has become my responsibility, you're under my protection until your husband's whereabouts are accounted for. I'm off duty until the day after Christmas. If we go to a motel, it won't have all the comforts of home and that's what you and your baby need. But it's your decision, Mrs. Sinclair."

He'd probably been up twenty-four hours straight by now and was dying to go home. Of course he was! But because of her, he couldn't unless she went there with him. This would be one small way to pay him back. "Then Jack and I would be very grateful to accept your hospitality, but only as long as you call me Andrea."

"That works both ways. The name's Flynn. While you get organized, I'll take Jack's car seat and install it in the back of my truck. I'll ask the nurse to wheel you out to the front doors of the hospital. See you in a few minutes."

FLYNN WALKED OUT to the parking area. Most of the cars had been cleaned off, but a few were still covered in snow. He scanned the lot for signs of a camper, but didn't see one. The storm front had moved on, leaving the sun trying to break through clouds.

While he warmed up the truck, he installed the car seat. As long as he was still alone, he called Nyall to let him know his plans and learned his boss had put out an APB on an older-model truck camper. Flynn asked him to get the police to check on the female flight attendant living in Albuquerque. Maybe Jerry Sinclair was with her, since they'd been involved for a long time.

They chatted a minute longer, then he drove around to the hospital's main doors. No sooner had he jumped down from the cab than he spied Andrea and the baby being pushed out in a wheelchair. With her hair the color of a fine white wine, he'd notice her anywhere.

"Perfect timing," she said as they met under the parapet. Her startling blue eyes smiled at him.

"I'll load Jack first."

"There you go, sweetheart." She handed him the baby.

He could smell her fragrance on the baby and his blanket. "Come on, little guy. We're going to my house."

Strapping him in was quite a different proposition from last night when he'd had to release him from his prison. As he went back for the diaper bag and suitcase, the baby started to cry.

"Uh-oh. Here—" She handed Flynn a baby toy from the diaper bag. "He likes this blue doughnut the best."

Flynn could understand why. Her son looked up into eyes that color all the hours he was awake. In a minute the baby was content and everything was loaded, including the attractive mother strapped in the front seat.

He forced himself to look away, needing to concentrate on his driving and watch for any truck campers she might recognize. "You're seeing Fort Davis under unusual conditions," he said after they'd taken off.

"So I gathered from the weather forecast yesterday. Considering the time of year, everyone got their surprise white Christmas. It looks pretty." She was staring out the side window. "To be honest, I've been dreading it since Thanksgiving."

If anyone could relate…

Lunchtime traffic on the main street had picked up. He pulled into a drive-through to get them a hamburger. Once they'd finished eating, he drove to the next corner and headed for the new housing development where he'd bought a small one-story house with vaulted ceilings. Flynn had chosen it for all the windows and the illusion of space. When he'd lost his family, every dream had been shattered and a light had gone out. Since then he'd had to depend on the sun to help him get up and face the next day.

"I've been gone three weeks, so let's hope my cleaning lady has been doing her job." He hadn't expected to wind up this last murder case until the New Year.

He pulled into the driveway and pressed the remote so they could enter the garage. Seeing his gray Volvo reminded him he hadn't driven it in over a month. When he went to the grocery store later, he'd take it to make sure it still ran.

After he shut off the engine, she turned to him. "I'm aware you weren't planning on company, so please don't apologize for anything. To be honest, I'm still trying to figure out how to repay you. Rest assured that one day I *will*."

Her sincerity touched a chord inside him. In fact, everything about her appealed to him. With her wavy blond hair framing classic features, she was a natural beauty. He found he couldn't take his eyes off her. The sound of the garage door closing alarmed the baby, who started to cry, breaking the moment that had Flynn spellbound.

He levered himself from the cab and went around to undo him. "Come here, buddy." It tickled him that when he held Jack against his chest, he stopped crying.

"My son was rescued by a Texas Ranger and now it appears you have the golden touch," Andrea said in a teasing voice. She'd come up behind him holding her purse and the diaper bag.

Flynn smiled before reaching for the blue doughnut that had fallen. "We'll see how long it lasts." He unlocked the door into the laundry-room area that led to the kitchen. Except for the cleaning lady and his family, no woman had crossed his threshold since he'd moved here. He'd never expected it could happen under any circumstances. What in heaven's name had possessed him?

ANDREA TOOK THE BABY from him and waited in the kitchen until he brought her suitcase in from the truck. Their eyes met.

"I love all the light! The furnished apartment I've been renting is in an old neighborhood where everything was built in the fifties. You know the style—California claustrophobic and cheap with that recessed lighting and heavy drapes. You can breathe here."

"I like it. In Houston, where I used to live, I also had a much older two-story house with more bedrooms and a big wooded yard, but a place that size is no longer necessary."

She heard the pain in his voice. "Well, this is lovely and looks brand-new." The walls were a creamy sand color with matching carpet throughout.

"I'll show you around."

She followed him to the open living room with its gas log fireplace. With a flick of the wall switch, he turned it on and it started throwing out heat.

Through the French doors she saw a den with a comfortable-looking leather couch and chairs. One part contained a table with computer equipment. On another wall stood an armoire with a television.

Farther on through the house she discovered two large-sized bedrooms at either end of the hall, each with its own bathroom. "My sisters decorated for me," he said. "They know I like traditional furnishings. This one with blue accent colors will be yours and the baby's while you're here."

He sounded as though she might be his responsibility for a while, but she didn't dare impose on him after tonight. "Thank you. I don't see a speck of dust. Looks like your cleaning lady has done a great job."

"I'll have to tell her. Now, while you two get settled,

I'm leaving to buy some groceries and a few items you'll need for Jack. Is that brand of formula the one you like best?" She nodded. "Good. I'll pick up some more and a bundle of disposable diapers."

"Flynn—I-I'd rather go to the store with you." Her voice faltered.

"You're supposed to be resting. Doctor's orders, remember? Don't worry. My house is under twenty-four-hour surveillance effective immediately. Your only concern should be to relax. I won't be long."

After tousling Jack's hair, he left. She retraced her steps to the living room and saw him back the Volvo down the driveway. The moment was surreal.

Andrea looked around, admiring the tasteful furniture and wall decor. Everything was beautiful, but it didn't feel lived in and she knew why….

One thing his house and her apartment had in common. There was no sign of Christmas.

Jerry had turned her world into such a nightmare, she'd forgotten what it was like to live an ordinary, happy life. As for Flynn, he didn't want to be reminded of what he'd lost. Yet in his grief, he'd reached out to her and Jack, knowing the joy she felt in being reunited with her son. He was such a good man.

"Come on, sweetheart. Let's go give you a bath and make you comfy." Ten minutes later Jack lay on his tummy on top of the bed and watched her while she talked to Sheila North on the phone.

"I've phoned your husband's attorney and explained the situation. He's supposed to get back to me after he's reached his client, but I haven't heard from him yet. Anything could be happening as we speak. I'm glad Captain Patterson has taken charge of your case. You'll be safe with him. Keep me posted, and hang in there."

"I will. Thanks, Sheila."

Andrea hung up and lay down alongside Jack, who'd fallen asleep. Thanks to Flynn, she knew she was safe.

Chapter Four

There were a bunch of Christmas trees for sale in front of the store. Flynn walked past them and went inside to grab a shopping cart and get busy.

"Hey, Flynn? What are you doing in the baby-care section?"

Uh-oh. He recognized his friend's voice and turned around. "How are you doing, Chuck?"

His rancher friend grinned. "I was about to ask you the same thing. It's been a month."

"I know. I was on a case out of town that lasted longer than I would have expected. Now I've been brought in on another case."

"So what gives with all the diapers and formula?"

In a low voice he said, "For the moment, I've got a family under witness protection." That was as close to the truth as he wanted to get. If anyone found out he had a gorgeous woman like Andrea staying under his roof, the news would spread among his friends like wildfire.

"A family with a baby, no less. That's tough, especially at Christmas. I guess you won't be making it to the Crandalls' on Christmas Eve."

"Afraid not."

"Well, give me a call when you're free and we'll do some serious riding."

"Sounds good. This will be over soon. See you later."

Hoping he wouldn't bump into anyone else he knew, Flynn went over to the food aisles and filled the shopping cart. On his way to the checkout stand, he passed the Christmas section. A display of frosted, colored lights flickered on and off, drawing his attention.

His little girl had been mesmerized by the flashing lights on their tree. Maybe Jack would like them, too. On a whim, he grabbed four boxes plus a Christmas tree skirt and put them in the cart.

Within fifteen minutes he had everything in the Volvo, including a Christmas tree with a wooden stand.

He had only a couple more things to get, so he drove to a store where he could purchase a fold-up playpen that could be made into a bed. He bought that and a carry-cot. Before he left the store, he'd also bought a baby quilt with blue and green hippos on it. When Andrea had fled New Mexico, she'd brought only the bare necessities with her.

On the way home, he checked with the guys on surveillance. All was quiet. He phoned his boss, who said the man who'd called 911 hadn't seen the camper truck, and neither had the convenience-mart clerk who'd been inside the store too busy to notice what was going on outside. Flynn was still waiting to hear back from Sheila North concerning Jerry Sinclair's whereabouts.

Checking with the hospital, he learned the patient still wasn't talking. That didn't surprise him. He'd wait until tomorrow when the suspect was taken to the jail in Marfa, then Flynn would try talking to him again. If the police had rounded up a public defender for him, then Flynn would encourage him to get his client to talk. For now he had nothing to do but go home and make things comfortable for his unexpected guests.

When he reached the house, he had to make four trips from the car to get everything inside. He stood the tree next to the fireplace, then went back in the kitchen to put the groceries away. Still no sound coming from the other part of the house. He finally picked up the box with the playpen and walked to the hallway.

Andrea had left the door open. The sight that greeted his eyes brought a lump to his throat. She was sound asleep on her side, still dressed in the clothes she'd worn home from the hospital. Little Jack was wide awake on his tummy with his head bobbing around, seemingly happy as could be.

Until now Flynn hadn't noticed that his eyes were blue like his mother's, but not quite as brilliant. The second the baby saw him in the doorway, he started to cry.

Flynn didn't know if he was frightened or wanted to be picked up. Whatever the reason, it brought Andrea awake. A cry of surprise escaped her lips. "I didn't know you were back—" She sat up, enchantingly disheveled, and reached for Jack.

"Sorry. I didn't mean to disturb you, but he saw me."

"I can't believe I fell asleep."

"You needed it. As long you're awake, I'll just set this up." Flynn opened the box with the playpen and started putting it together as a bed. Luckily it wasn't too complicated. He had to look at the instructions only twice. That was a good thing, since he needed to keep busy before she caught him staring. Her face and womanly shape made too tempting a picture.

She slid off the bed holding Jack. "I can't believe you've gone to so much trouble. You shouldn't have done it. I hope we'll be able to leave tomorrow."

"I wouldn't plan on it until after Christmas. We know nothing about your husband's activities or his involvement in this situation. Until we do, keeping you and the baby safe is the first priority." He glanced at Jack. "That little guy does a lot of moving and needs his own bed."

"Then let me pay you for it."

"It's Christmas. I felt like buying him some presents." Flynn couldn't believe he'd said that. "There's a pack of diapers and formula on the kitchen counter. Go ahead and take what you need. Make yourself at home. He sounds like he's hungry."

"Thank you," she said in a quiet voice. "Come on, Jack. Let's go warm a bottle for you."

Flynn lifted his head. "He drank it cold for me last night. Your son's a real trouper." At that remark, an unguarded smile broke out on her face. Something about it warmed places inside him that hadn't seen the sunshine in two years.

A few minutes later, from the other part of the house, he heard her cry, "You bought a tree, too?" It was a happy sound. He was glad he'd gone to the trouble. After he took the quilt out of the sack and draped it over the side of the playpen, he gathered up the mess and headed for the garage.

As he passed her in the kitchen, he noticed she'd taken the top off the bottle to warm it in the microwave. "How do tacos sound for dinner later? I bought a ton of groceries."

"Anything sounds good." By now she'd found a kitchen chair and had started feeding Jack.

When he'd put the box out in the garbage and had come in again, she said, "Can I ask you one more favor?"

He washed his hands. "Name it."

"Will you please forget about us and take care of yourself now? I happen to know you were already up a long time before you came across the accident scene. You need twelve hours of sleep at least."

"I'll admit I could use a few."

"I thought so. Let's not worry about dinner right now. I'll find myself something to eat when I want to snack. Jack and I will play in front of the TV and have a great time. If you should wake up before I'm in bed, I'll fix *your* dinner. That way I won't feel like I'm an ungrateful guest."

He flicked her a glance. "You're the kind of guest I could get used to." Again, he didn't know where the comment had come from. "If you're sure."

"Positive."

"The next time I'm up, I'll string the Christmas lights. They flash on and off. My daughter was fascinated by them."

Her mouth lifted at one corner. "No doubt Jack will be hypnotized. Now, do yourself a favor and go to bed before you pass out on your feet."

"I look that bad, do I?"

"Do you want an honest answer to that question?" she teased.

She's getting to you, Flynn. As the guys would say, Andrea Sinclair had slipped in under the radar. He sucked in his breath. "If something comes up, promise you won't hesitate to wake me?"

"Cross my heart."

"All right, then." Calling on his self-control, which was practically nonexistent at this point, he resisted the urge to give them both a kiss before he left the kitchen.

After a shower and a shave, he was halfway gone and diving for the bed when his cell phone rang. He had to answer it.

"Yes?"

"It's Nyall. The police in Carlsbad can't find Jerry Sinclair or his Audi. He called in sick yesterday, so he didn't have to show up for his flight. There's an APB out on him. I've put extra security on your house in case he's lurking around here. Watch your back."

"Will do. Thanks for the update."

He pulled the covers over himself and didn't know anything else until his phone rang again. When he reached for it, he saw that it was quarter to ten. He'd slept a full eight hours! After checking the caller ID, he clicked on. It was his sister.

"Bethany?"

"Hi. I know it's getting late, but Kaye and I haven't heard from you in weeks and just wondered how you're doing. Where are you?"

"Home in bed. How's everybody at your house?"

"Better now that I'm talking to you."

His sisters worried about him too much. "I'm on a case right now." One he'd never seen coming.

"Okay, I'll let you go, but remember if you need anything at all, call us."

"I always do."

"No, you don't. We all love you, Flynn."

"I love you, too. Did you get the boxes I sent?"

"Yes. Kaye came over for hers. Ours is sitting under the tree."

"Give the kids a hug from their Uncle Flynn."

"How about giving them one yourself by coming to Houston?"

"Can't right now."

"You always say that." He heard a troubled sigh. "I won't keep you any longer. Love you." She clicked off.

His sisters were the best, but right now his mind was on Andrea. Hoping she wasn't asleep yet, he levered himself from the bed and hurried into the bathroom. After dressing in jeans and a favorite white polo, he headed down the dark hall for the living room.

And what to his wondering eyes should he see, but a gorgeous elf putting the last of the flashing lights on the tree.

Jack lay on his back on top of the quilt Flynn had bought. She'd spread it out on the carpet next to her while she worked. His arms and legs were going ninety miles an hour, as if he was trying to reach the lights.

"It looks like Santa's helpers sneaked in while I was sleeping."

Andrea gave a little gasp of surprise. For once he thought she might be staring at him. Damn if he didn't hope she liked what she saw. "You're up! What do you think?"

"I think you're hired."

Her chuckle delighted him. "I knew you were so exhausted, the last thing you'd want to do is put up lights. I hope you don't mind. After I woke up from my second nap today, it gave me something to do, and it has helped me unwind. My little sidekick has been coaching me."

She had a way of putting things that made him want to smile. "Mind if I hold him?"

"He's looking at you right now. I think if you don't, he's going to cry."

"Well, we can't have that now, can we?" So saying, he scooped him up from the floor and kissed his cheeks. "Do you know your baby has the cutest face I ever saw?"

Her hands stilled on the Christmas skirt she was putting around the base of the tree. "Your little girl takes the honors there, but Jack and I aren't complaining. How about you show us a picture of her and her mommy."

He clutched the baby tightly against his chest. The moment had come to pull it out of the dresser drawer and take a look.

"Come with me, Jack."

ANDREA HAD TAKEN a calculated risk, but she wanted to know more about Flynn's life. He was her guardian angel right now. He spent his life keeping other people safe, but she felt he instinctively guarded his heart. The hunger she saw in him when he held Jack revealed how devastated he'd been to lose his wife and child. Maybe if he talked about it a little bit it would help him to get through this painful time.

When he came back into the room with a framed photograph, she took it from him without saying anything. Both his wife and daughter were brunettes and utterly adorable. How did anyone ever get over that kind of loss?

"They're beautiful. Thank you for showing this to me." She lifted her eyes to Flynn. "You've been a daddy. No wonder you seem so comfortable with Jack." She handed the photo back to him. "Was she a good baby?"

"Easy. Perfect."

"Of course. Were you and your wife happy?"

He nodded slowly.

"Then you were a very blessed man, even if your time with them was cut short."

Flynn put the picture on the coffee table before turning back to her. "I'm sorry you've had trouble in your marriage."

"So am I. When I first met Jerry, I thought *This is the one.* If there were warning signs, I didn't see them. I'd dated quite a lot over the years, so that when he came along, he stood out from everyone else. Because he was a pilot we had our time apart, but when we came together it was like a honeymoon every time."

She looked at the floor. "What I didn't know was that when he was away flying, he was having a honeymoon with other women on his layovers. Like that old saying about the sailor with a wife in every port, that was Jerry."

Flynn's features sobered. "He's the loser now. Not you. You have your son and can get on with a brand-new life full of all sorts of possibilities."

Andrea bit her lip. "I'm sure your loved ones have told you the same thing, that life is out there ready for you to embrace. But we both know it's a lot easier said than done."

"Touché. Once you've loved, it's hard to let it go no matter what," he said in his deep voice.

Her gaze turned to his. "He's not the man I thought he was, so that pain is gone. In my case it's the dream that's been hard to get over."

"In time you'll heal, especially when you know you don't have anything more to fear from him after he's caught."

"What do you think will happen?"

"He'll be arraigned. In all probability the judge will order psychiatric testing before he hands down sentencing. Even if he had nothing to do with the attempted kidnapping, he has harassed you and violated the restraining order many times. But if he is implicated, then a trial date will be set with a jury and witnesses."

She bowed her head. "As long as he can't hurt Jack…"

"Amen."

This conversation had gone on long enough. It was time to change the subject. "While you were sleeping,

I fixed dinner and ate mine. Yours is in the fridge. All I have to do is warm it up. If you'll entertain Jack for a minute more, I'll put it on the kitchen table."

"Terrific. We'll just examine the tree up close and decide what kind of ornaments we want to put on it."

Through the open space between the living room and kitchen she said, "Do you have any?"

"No. After the funeral, my family helped me move here. I told my sisters to take anything they wanted. I'll buy some more."

She nodded. "I did virtually the same thing in my haste to get away from Jerry. In order not to have anything to do with him, I just walked out and left it all for him except a few of my own belongings. The furnished apartment saved my life."

"They have their uses. Many's the time I've had to use one on a long stakeout." He wandered into the kitchen. "Umm. You made tacos. They smell good."

"Help yourself." She walked over and took Jack from him. "While you eat, I'm going to put him down. I can see his eyelids drooping."

Flynn gave him a kiss on top of his head. "See you in the morning, little guy."

"I'll say good-night, too." She reached for the bottle she'd warmed. "My thanks will never be enough for what you're doing for us."

Afraid she might break down, she headed for the bedroom, picking up the quilt off the living-room floor as she did so. As much as she wanted to stay and talk with Flynn while he ate, she decided it would be better to keep everything professional between them. After his kindness to her, the last thing he wanted was some needy, clingy woman waiting on his every word. She imagined every eligible female for miles had their eye on him.

Jack went down without a fuss, allowing her to get ready for bed and slide under the covers. When she'd been shoved into the snow, she couldn't have dreamed she'd end up in this man's home being totally cared for. She admired him more than anyone she knew.

While she lay there, it suddenly dawned on her that for the first time in ages she was finding her thoughts focused on someone other than herself and Jack. Her heart ached for the man in the other part of the house who'd lost the two most important people in his life. They now had faces. Had it been a mistake to ask him to see their picture? She feared it had dredged up the pain he'd tried so hard to suppress.

Scalding tears she couldn't hold back trickled out of the corners of her eyes onto the pillow.

Chapter Five

Andrea was a great cook. Flynn ate everything with relish and put his dishes in the dishwasher, but he was wide awake after his long sleep and wouldn't want bed for a while. Deciding he was too wired to be this inactive, he turned off the gas fire and left for the store. With security outside watching the house, he could leave without worry.

He had twenty minutes before it closed. In that amount of time he could pick out some ornaments. By the time he'd put them on the tree, he might be ready to go back to bed.

But to his chagrin, an hour later all the activity still hadn't tired him out. Once he'd climbed under the bedding, he lay awake for a long time thinking about the woman at the other end of the hall. Jack wasn't the only person in this house who'd gotten to him.

Surprisingly, he didn't awaken until nine the next morning, evidence he was still catching up on lost sleep. He could smell bacon cooking. It appeared his house guest liked to stay busy, too. It took him back to weekend mornings with Michelle.

Flynn rolled out of bed and stretched before heading to the bathroom. When he looked in the mirror, it hit him what was different about this morning. He no longer experienced that stabbing pain of loss that had always been there since the plane crash.

The psychiatrist had told him there'd come a day when he'd realize he was healing and life started to look good to him again. His doctor had said it would sneak up on him when he least expected it because the mind and heart took their own sweet time.

That was a fact.

Maybe it was finding Jack alive and uniting him with his mother that had done the trick. Whatever dynamic had been in play, it had helped him turn a corner. The Jack Daniel's would stay on the shelf untouched this holiday.

Before anything else, he called the hospital and learned the patient had been released and transferred to Marfa. Since he'd be driving there in a little while, he discarded the idea of relaxing in his new pair of sweats and put on a blue-and-red plaid flannel shirt and jeans. Once he'd pulled on his boots, he made his way through the house to the living room filled with warmth from the fireplace.

Andrea sat crossed-legged in front of the tree with Jack at her side. This time she looked breathtaking dressed in a long-sleeved navy turtleneck and jeans. Her baby lay on his back on the quilt while she teased him with some plastic toy keys. The whole time she made him reach for them, his excited body was in perpetual motion. He wore a smile on his precious face that tugged at Flynn's heart.

"I can see the Christmas elf has been at it again," he drawled. Without thinking about it, he sat down on the other side of the baby and leaned over to kiss him.

Her brilliant blue eyes lit up when she saw him. "Well, good morning! After putting all these shiny new ornaments on the tree by yourself, we thought you might sleep in until noon at least. You must have been up half the night. Are you hungry?"

"Starving."

"Good. I put your breakfast in the oven to stay warm."

His lips twitched before he got to his feet. "No wonder Santa's so jolly and plump." Suddenly in the Christmas mood, Flynn headed for the den and turned on the radio to a music station playing Christmas music. With the sound of "Jingle Bell Rock" filtering through the house, he headed for the kitchen.

Equipped with scrambled eggs, bacon and hash browns, he grabbed a fork and went back to his spot in front of the tree. While he sat down to eat, Jack watched him with attentive blue eyes. "I know your milk tastes good to you, but it's nothing like this. Just wait until you can eat your mom's cooking. You'll flip!"

"Flynn…"

He flashed her a quick grin. "It's only the truth." After putting his empty plate to the side he turned over on his stomach so he could look Jack in the eye. "Hey, buddy—what do you want to do today? How about after I come back from the jail, we watch a fun cartoon on TV and give your mom a break?"

Andrea eyed him furtively. "I'm sure Jack would love it, but if you're going to the jail, could we go with you? I'd like to talk to the man who stole my car yesterday."

Just like that, the mood had changed. For a little while Flynn had forgotten everything, including the reason she'd spent the night under his roof. "It's not normally allowed, and you're supposed to be getting your rest today."

"I've done nothing but relax since you brought me to

your home twenty-four hours ago. I'd only talk to him for a few minutes. If Jerry hired him, I want to know how he paid him of my hard-earned money. I bought and paid for my own cars and would like to hear how he's going to pay me back for the one he crashed."

Flynn couldn't blame her for that. Not only had the creep terrified her by stealing her baby, her only transportation was gone. He was enraged for her in his own right.

"I'll take you, but pack a few extras for Jack. The jail is in Marfa, twenty-four miles from here. No telling how long we'll be. Depending on the situation and the attorney defending him, you might be able to have a few minutes with him. Let's leave now and get it over with. Then we'll have the rest of the day to enjoy ourselves."

He watched her swallow hard. "Thank you, Flynn. I'll get Jack ready."

While she stood up and took the baby back to the bedroom, he shut off the radio and gas fire. After slipping on his parka, he took advantage of his privacy and phoned security outside to let them know his plans.

Once he'd hung up, he reached the garage ahead of her and changed the baby's car seat to the rear of the Volvo. When he saw her in the doorway, he reached for Jack and settled him in. "Here we go, buddy. I think you'll like riding in this better than in the truck, where it's hard to see around the seats."

ANDREA MARVELED OVER Flynn's concern for her son's welfare. *And mine.* He treated her like a princess. That's how she felt on this beautiful Christmas Eve day. Even the sun had come out to warm the air and a lot of the snow had already melted.

Two days ago she'd been running for her life through

an unexpected blizzard, straight into a kidnapper's clutches. This morning she could truly breathe again. The sorrow and fear she'd been living with since the last months of her pregnancy no longer held her in a vise. The remarkable man at her side was the person solely responsible for this change.

If she felt any alarm, it was her own growing attraction to him. She couldn't blame it on hero worship, although she did think he was a hero. No…this was another feeling taking over despite her determination to stay emotionally distanced from him.

Once they were on the highway, Andrea asked him to tell her about the murder case in Van Horn. Talking about his work would help keep her focused on his profession rather than on him. "I've discovered you're famous. The story is all over the news, and the staff at the hospital sang your praises."

"Don't believe it. A whole network was involved to get the job done."

"With *you* spearheading it," she reminded him. "Don't you see? This will be the only time in my life I actually have an opportunity to learn the facts from the horse's mouth—so to speak."

His deep laughter excited her. "That about covers it."

"Flynn—"

He shook his head. "You don't want to hear the gruesome details."

Modesty wasn't the only thing holding him back. Something in his tone made her realize he didn't want to revisit it. That's probably how he'd survived since going into law enforcement. Put it away and move on to another case.

"I'm sorry. It's just that because of what you do, I got

my son back, and I know you're going to see that Jerry no longer poses a threat. I'm pretty much in awe of you."

While she studied his distinctive profile, he gave her a rueful smile. "That sounds good, but I'll wait until the job is successfully done before I take those words to heart."

She had no doubts, but unfortunately she'd been caught looking at him again. With her pulse racing, Andrea turned away and discovered they were coming into Marfa. In a minute they drove up to the Presidio County Jail, a one-story building.

"We've arrived and there hasn't been a peep out of Jack."

Andrea looked over her shoulder. "A drive usually puts him to sleep."

"I'm afraid snooze time is over for the little guy. The jail is a busy, noisy place with visitors coming and going. Let me carry him in for you."

Flynn got out to take care of Jack while she gathered the diaper bag and they walked inside. He'd been right. There were a dozen people in the lounge area obviously waiting to visit detainees. One young woman, who was maybe twenty, held a crying baby. Two of the adults were having an argument and didn't seem to care if anyone heard them. On the day before Christmas, the reality of the situation was all the more depressing.

After kissing Jack's forehead, Flynn handed her the baby. "Sit down over here while I go in and find out what's going on. After I come back out, I'll tend Jack so you can have a turn. That is *if* they let you."

"Be careful—" she said before she realized how stupid and personal it sounded.

His eyes turned that soft gray color again. "That was nice to hear. It's been a long time."

She could feel herself blushing. "It just came out. I don't know why I said it."

He studied her for a second longer. "I promise not to be long." He headed for a door marked Authorized Personnel Only.

The woman with the baby walked over to her. "I need to change my kid. Do you have an extra diaper?"

"Sure." Andrea dug in the bag for one.

"I'm here to see my boyfriend. He got busted last night for getting in a fight. What about you?"

Andrea handed her a diaper and some wipes. "I'm here to talk to a man who was brought in from the hospital."

"What did he do?"

"He kidnapped my baby, but a Texas Ranger caught him."

The woman's painted brows arched. "You're talking about the stud who walked in here with you?"

Flynn *was* a stud, and so much more, there weren't enough words to describe him. "Yes."

"Kind of reminds me of the hunk on the pack of cigarettes my grandad used to smoke. You know, the Marlboro Man?"

Andrea knew and nodded.

The younger woman eyed her for a moment longer before she took off for the restroom. No sooner had she disappeared than Flynn came striding into the lounge, the essence of the man the younger mother had been describing.

Andrea had thought he would have been gone a lot longer. Her heart thudded at the sight of him. Jack recognized him at once and squirmed to be held by him.

She laughed. "Look at that! My son's a traitor."

Flynn's eyes smiled as he reached for the baby. After

putting him against his shoulder he said, "While this case is still unfolding, I can't get permission for you to talk to him. Not until after he's arraigned by the federal court judge."

"Why? I only want to ask him a few questions."

"I know, but as I suspected, he wasn't working alone. The guy driving the truck camper was an accomplice and is still on the loose. The police have an APB out on him. Once he's caught, then you'll get your turn to talk to both of them."

"How did you find out this much?"

"After he refused to talk to me at the hospital, I gave instructions he could be allowed one phone call. The sheriff told me he made it to a P.I. firm he works for in Carlsbad. He goes by the name Stanley Cooper."

"He's a P.I.?" Andrea asked incredulously.

"No. He's someone they keep on the payroll to do certain kinds of dirty jobs for the firm. They've sent down their attorney, who has advised his client to remain silent."

Once again she was outraged. "And Jerry found them…"

"It goes without saying they're a sleazy outfit." He sounded thoughtful before he added, "This case is turning into something bigger than anyone had supposed."

"In what way?"

"My boss just got word back to me that the fingerprints I had sent to the database on the patient have identified him as Cooper Stanley, an alias he uses. He's done jail time before. At the moment there's a warrant out for a Cooper Stanley in Arizona for grand theft and shooting an officer."

Andrea shuddered. "Jerry must have paid a lot of

money for that firm to agree to kidnapping Jack. Where did he get it?"

Flynn grimaced. She noticed he had such a strong instinct to protect, he unconsciously held Jack tighter. "I can tell you this much. That place is going to be out of business and several people, including your husband, are going to be behind bars before too much longer." He looked her square in the eye. "Grab your things and let's go."

Relieved to get out of such a depressing place, she followed him through the main doors of the jail to his car. A few minutes later he pulled up in front of a restaurant called the Food Shark and shut off the engine.

"I'm ready for lunch. Let's go in. The chef serves slow-roasted pork tacos in an ancho-cocoa rub I know you'll like. We'll take some of their famous brown butter cookies to eat on the way home."

"Sounds delicious. Let me just change Jack and feed him a bottle, then he'll be good while we're inside."

"He's always good."

"That's because he's used to you and enjoys all the attention you shower on him. He's getting spoiled."

Flynn's eyes penetrated hers. "Don't you know every guy likes to be spoiled once in a while?"

"Just as long as he doesn't get in the habit. Within a few days, we'll have to leave."

A shadow fell over his rugged features. "I wouldn't plan on it being that soon."

"Then I'll move to a motel. You told me you go back on duty the day after Christmas."

"I don't think you understand. I'll be working your case until everything's tied up and you're safe. Until further notice, you're my responsibility and my house is the best place for you."

She averted her eyes. "Flynn—that could mean more than a few days."

"It could. But let's not worry about it. You have no family, no job. Do you still have the furnished apartment to return to?"

"No. I paid the last month's rent when I left."

"Then there's no problem with you staying under my roof."

"There's a big problem," she fired back. "When people find out, they'll talk."

"They do anyway, so let them. They know nothing about what you've been through, but I do. That's all that's important here."

The ring of steel in his tone sent a shiver down her spine. There were times he could be so tender, she wanted to cry. But there were other times like now when the tough Ranger in him took over.

He hadn't been able to save his own wife and child, but she sensed he had a vested interest in Jack since finding him in the storm. She knew he would do whatever was necessary to make him and her secure for as long as need be. Deep down inside, Andrea had to admit she loved that quality in Flynn.

"If I'm going to stay, then I need something worthwhile to do to earn my keep."

"Let me think about it." He didn't sound as stern as before. "If you want to know the truth, I'm glad you weren't able to talk to the prisoner. You're a good-looking woman. Cooper would have baited you for the sheer enjoyment of it. Nothing would have been accomplished except to add to your stress."

"You're probably right about his being cruel."

You're a good-looking woman.

He'd paid her a compliment in a context he would

have used with any woman he was protecting to put a point across. Was there anything personal behind it? She didn't know.

But there was a part of her that wanted to think it was personal. *Isn't that right, you foolish girl?*

Chapter Six

Full of good food, Andrea relaxed as they headed back to Fort Davis. She couldn't believe she'd developed feelings for Flynn already. The more time she spent with him, the worse she knew it was going to get. Somehow she had to find a way to hide her emotions.

Changing the subject, she said, "Do you have any movies we could watch after we get home?"

"My favorite is in my stuff somewhere. I haven't seen it in years."

"Then it's an oldie?"

"Yes, but still post-Jurassic," he said in a teasing tone. To her relief he sounded more lighthearted again. They drove into Fort Davis and before long reached the house.

Flynn seemed to love taking care of Jack, so she didn't say anything as he carried him inside. When they reached the living room, he put him down on his back. "It feels good to stretch, doesn't it, buddy?"

Jack was wide awake, full of excitement. He watched Flynn flip the switch for the gas fire and turn on the tree lights. His blue eyes followed the master of the house everywhere he went. The touching scene caught her off guard, causing her eyes to smart.

To her dismay Flynn trapped her gaze and couldn't

have helped but notice she'd teared up. "Are you all right?"

She wiped the tears away with her fingers. "I'm just so grateful to you."

He sobered. "That works both ways. On the way back from Van Horn the other night, the thought of coming home to this empty house was unbearable. Having you here is a gift to me, so that makes us even."

Andrea believed him and nodded. "I'll be back in a minute." She walked into the bedroom to take off her coat and freshen up. When she returned, Flynn got up from the floor where he'd been playing with Jack.

"I'm going down to the basement to hunt for my box of old DVDs. Don't go away."

The second he started to leave, Jack began crying. She reached for the baby to comfort him, then turned to Flynn. "Did you hear that? You've got an admirer. Don't be too long or we may have a disaster on our hands."

He smiled at her from the kitchen. "Hang in there, Jack!"

She carried him around the room and they looked out the front windows until Flynn returned. "That was fast."

"My sisters marked all the cartons during the move. That made it easy." He opened a shoe box and filed through the disks. "Ah—here it is." He handed it to her.

A Christmas Story. Her eyes flew to his. "This is my favorite, too. I fell in love with Ralphie. He was the cutest boy I ever saw. It never felt like he was acting."

Flynn nodded. "He was like every kid who ever wanted one special thing for Christmas and he wanted that Red Ryder BB gun. I was seven years old at the time this movie came out. When his dad finally told him to look behind the desk for his present, I bawled my eyes out."

"So did I. Did that movie sow the seeds for you to become a Texas Ranger?"

"Probably that and a dozen other reasons."

"Like what?"

"There was a murder case in Houston involving an employee at my father's insurance agency. The police bungled it and it took several years before the killer was caught. I was so sure I could have handled it better, I decided to go into law enforcement."

She eyed him for a brief moment. "Have you solved all the cases you've been given?"

He rubbed the side of his hard jaw. "No. There must be half a dozen cold ones sitting in my files. They haunt me."

"I'm sure they do, but since it's Christmas Eve, let's only think happy thoughts. I'm one person who can testify you're the best of the best. For as long as I live, I'll never forget what you've done for me and Jack." She gave him back the DVD. "Now it's time to put my baby down for a his big nap."

"So soon?" Flynn actually sounded disappointed.

"He's not going to like being away from you, but if he stays on his routine he won't get cranky. You don't want to know what that's like."

"Mother knows best." He kissed Jack's temple. In the process Flynn's cheek brushed hers. She knew it was by accident, but rivulets of magmalike heat worked their way through her body. "While you settle him, I have an errand to run, then we'll get down to some serious movie watching."

WHILE FLYNN WAS MAKING a few purchases, his cell phone rang. When he saw the caller ID, he walked to the end of the aisle where he could talk in private and clicked on. “What have you got for me, Nyall?”

“Plenty. Stanley Cooper said you told him you would cut him a deal with the judge if he told you what he knew, so he fingered the guy who was driving the camper. His name is Ray Hollis. The police picked him up at his rooming house in Carlsbad. The camper belongs to the P.I. firm. I talked to the police chief there and learned they’re investigating the owners as we speak.”

“Good. That’s a few less vermin off the streets. What else?”

“Your instincts were right on about Sinclair.”

He gripped his phone tighter. “What do you mean?”

“The police found him hiding out at his girlfriend’s apartment in Albuquerque. He’s been arrested and transported to the jail in Carlsbad.”

“They run to type, don’t they?”

Flynn should have been elated to learn that the husband who’d made Andrea’s life a living hell had been captured. But he knew that the moment he told her Jack’s father was in custody, everything was going to change. When he thought of her leaving and taking the baby with her, his body broke out in a cold sweat. He wasn’t ready for that yet.

“You’re free to interrogate him, but Flynn—it’s Christmas. I’m ordering you to try to enjoy it before you leave for Carlsbad.”

The second Nyall mentioned Sinclair, tight bands had constricted Flynn’s lungs and still wouldn’t let go, but he answered, “That’s one order I intend to obey.”

After a surprised pause, Nyall asked, “Since when?”

Since you don’t want to know and I can’t tell you.

“Like you said, it’s Christmas.”

Nyall would have assumed that after Andrea had been released from the hospital, Flynn would have made arrangements for her to sort out her life while she stayed at the women's shelter in Alpine where she'd been headed. But something earthshaking had happened to Flynn and he wasn't about to explain why he'd caused things to go in a different direction.

The security Flynn had hired to keep a watch out for Sinclair was strictly private and paid for with his own money, not public taxpayers' dollars. The two retired police officers who could use the additional income knew better than to make a peep about this. Now that Flynn no longer required security for Andrea and Jack, he needed to let the officers know, but he'd phone them when he got back to his car. As for Andrea, Flynn had no more excuses to keep her with him and needed to come up with another plan.

Fifteen minutes later he pulled into the garage. He'd made up his mind about one thing—if she asked him any questions about her case tonight, of course he would have to tell her the news.

But if fate was kind and she enjoyed the movies until she went to bed, then he wouldn't say anything until tomorrow after they'd enjoyed Christmas and she'd opened her presents. Knowing her husband had been arrested would be his final gift to her. They'd go from there, because he'd made up his mind she and Jack weren't leaving Fort Davis for a while.

No sooner did he walk into the house with his packages than she met him in the kitchen looking worried. "I'm glad you're back."

His dark brows furrowed. "Is there something wrong with Jack?"

"No. He should stay asleep until his eight-o'clock

bottle. You need to know your house phone rang a while ago and I heard the message. Someone named—Tonto?—said he was coming by the house at six to see you and bring you a present."

Flynn chuckled. He might have known Chuck's curiosity couldn't leave things alone. He'd realized something was up when he'd caught Flynn buying baby formula. No doubt he'd gotten on the phone to their friend Riley. It wouldn't surprise him if they both showed up.

Andrea looked flustered. "It's almost that time now. If you didn't get here soon, I didn't know whether to answer the door or pretend no one was here. I turned off the Christmas tree lights just in case."

"Don't be nervous. He's a good friend who runs a saddlery shop here in Fort Davis. I have a gift for him, too. When I moved here, he offered to let me board my horse at his ranch and we became friends. When he checks fences, I ride with him if I have the time."

"That sounds wonderful. It must be very relaxing for you."

"I love it. Have you ever ridden?"

"A few times at a riding stable with friends when I was a lot younger. It was fun."

Maybe he could do something to put a little more fun like that into her life. "Give me a minute to put these sacks in the bedroom, then we'll celebrate with the treats I bought. Do you want to find some cups? There's a tray in that bottom cupboard on the left."

He left the food sitting on the counter. Before going to his bedroom, he turned the Christmas tree lights back on. Later on, after she went to bed, he'd wrap the gifts he'd just bought and put them under the tree.

On his way back to the living room, he grabbed the

presents he'd purchased a few days ago for Riley and Chuck. He'd planned to leave them on their doorsteps tomorrow, but it seemed that effort would no longer be necessary. After turning on some Christmas music, he joined her in the kitchen.

"Have you tasted the cheese ball?"

Andrea gave him a guilty smile. "It's nummy." She'd arranged everything on a tray with the crackers. He picked up a cup of eggnog and drank some.

"This is really good. What did you sprinkle on the top?"

"Nutmeg."

"*That's* the reason. I didn't know I even had any. My sisters are nothing if not thorough."

"It's clear they love you."

"The feeling's mutual. I take it you were an only child."

"Yes. My parents died in a car accident when I was seventeen. I went to live with my great-aunt until she died."

"That must have been very rough." His husky-sounding comment coincided with the ringing of the doorbell. Flynn finished off the rest of his drink. "I'll get it." He headed for the front entry hall and opened the door. Sure enough, his two buddies stood there with gifts.

Chuck knew that Flynn wouldn't have answered the door if the witness-protection excuse was on the up and up. That's why his grin was broader than usual. Oddly enough, Flynn had told his friend the truth at the store, but it came with a unique twist that had a stranglehold on him.

"Merry Christmas!"

"The same back to you. Come on in and meet Andrea. She and her son are under my protection for a little while."

Their smiling eyes relayed private messages before they put their gifts under the tree.

"Guys? I'd like you to meet Andrea Sinclair from Carlsbad, New Mexico." They walked over to the coffee table. He saw their eyes ignite with male interest as he made the introductions. "Help yourself to some Christmas cheer and sit down for a while."

"Don't mind if I do," Chuck murmured.

"I take it you two are headed for the Crandalls' party."

Riley nodded. "Our families are meeting us there. But we decided to take a little detour in the hope of talking you into coming with us. You missed it last year. Bring Andrea and the baby with you. The more the merrier."

She shook her head. "I couldn't, but you go, Flynn."

In the background he heard the baby. Chuck's eyebrows lifted. "Uh-oh. Sorry. I guess the bell woke him."

"I'll see to him," Flynn said, anticipating Andrea's next move. "You need a break. Stay with our guests and I'll bring him out so the guys can meet him."

He left for his bedroom and opened one of the boxes. Inside was a little red Christmas stretchy suit and a red hat with white trim and a white snowball on the top. By the time he walked into the other bedroom, Jack had worked himself up, not liking to be ignored.

"Hey, it's okay, buddy. I've come to rescue you." Flynn picked him up and kissed him until he quieted down. Then he changed his diaper and put the new suit on him. "I was going to give this to you in the morning, but I think doing this now is even better. Let's see how this hat looks on you. Some good friends of mine are waiting to meet you."

As those blue eyes reminiscent of Andrea's stared so sweetly at him from beneath the hat's white trim, Flynn felt his heart melt. He grabbed a bottle of formula and carried the baby into the living room. "Guys? Meet Jack Sinclair. He's come straight from the North Pole."

"Oh, Flynn—" Andrea's cry among the guys' comments contained all the emotion he could have hoped for. The light from the tree glinted in her tear-filled eyes. She looked so beautiful, he could hardly breathe. He had to force himself to look at the others.

"I think Jack could win the cutest three-month-old of the year award, don't you? This little dude wanted to join in the fun, but he's still underage for eggnog."

His friends cracked up. With wide grins, they took turns holding him. They were fathers themselves and got a big kick out of this. Flynn pulled out his phone to take pictures. Jack didn't like it and reached for Andrea. That gave him more opportunities to catch the precious moment on camera. She sat down on the couch to comfort him.

"Something tells me he's hungry. Here you go, buddy." Flynn handed Andrea the bottle so she could feed him. Within seconds, peace reigned.

Turning to his friends he said, "More eggnog, anyone?"

Riley smiled. "Thanks, but we'd better get going."

Chuck glanced at Andrea with a more serious expression. "If it weren't for the other party, we'd rather stay and find out why you've come to be under the Lone Ranger's protection. In case you didn't know, that's a little joke between the three of us."

Andrea smiled at him. "I get it, *Tonto*."

Everyone laughed before Flynn handed them their gifts and saw them to the door. "Later, guys."

As the two of them started to walk away, Flynn heard their exchange.

"I'd say he probably won't come out of there before the spring thaw. What do you think?"

"It might even be Easter."

Filled with a newfound warmth, Flynn shut the door, no longer recognizing himself. This wasn't the same world he'd been living in three days ago....

EARLIER, WHEN FLYNN HAD been checking on the baby, Andrea had noticed Chuck walking around while Riley kept her entertained. The scoundrel had actually taped some mistletoe to the doorjamb between the living room and the den. She liked Flynn's fun-loving friends a lot, but she wasn't about to be caught in their latest little joke.

While he was saying good-night to them at the door, she carried Jack into the study and sat down on the farthest end of the couch to finish feeding him.

"Andrea?"

"In the den! We're waiting for you to start the movie."

"Which one do you want to see first?"

"Surprise us."

Flynn brought in the cheese and crackers. If he noticed the green sprig hanging down he didn't let on. As he inserted the disk, she watched him, all six foot three of him. No male of her acquaintance could fill a flannel shirt and jeans the way he did. When he sat down next to her, Andrea felt a surge of desire for him that shot aching pains to the palms of her hands.

Stunned by this reaction, she put the baby over her shoulder and pressed her face into his neck to get herself under control. When she finally dared lift her head, she saw Ralphie's house on the TV screen. Part of the delight of the film was the narrator's voice, making the story about a boy's heart being set on that Red Ryder gun come alive. Once again she felt the magic of it spread through her, drawing her in. Flynn was so engrossed, he kept munching on the snacks.

When it came to the part where Ralphie found his gun, they both turned to look at each other. "Gets to you every time, doesn't it."

"Yes. One day this will be Jack's favorite movie, too."

Flynn used the remote to pause the film. "Why don't we take a break. His eyelids are fluttering. While you put him to bed, I'll make us some sandwiches."

"That sounds like an excellent idea." Before he moved, she jumped up with the baby and hurried through the doorway to her bedroom.

The red suit was so cute, but she wanted to save it for morning. After pulling a light green one from the drawer, she got him ready for bed and sang to him. Once he'd fallen off, she tiptoed out of the room and made her way to the den.

Flynn was just putting the plate of sandwiches and drinks on the coffee table when he saw her. Revelation flowed through her that he'd seen the mistletoe. The look of silvery fire coming from his eyes caused the blood to pound in her ears, but he didn't make a move toward her.

With her heart slamming against her ribs, now would be the time to douse the flames and go back to her room, but another revelation came on top of the first one. She wanted the kiss to happen. She wanted it to happen more than anything she'd ever wanted in her whole life.

Like Ralphie, who'd seen the gun in the store window and had to have one just like it, she'd seen the long, dark, handsome Texas Ranger from her hospital bed. In the instant he'd told her he'd found Jack, a feeling had grabbed her that wouldn't let go. Three days later she was half crazy with wanting him in all the ways a woman wanted a man.

"I think you know my friends didn't need to put up the mistletoe."

At those words she sucked in her breath. "If we're being honest, I'd hoped it wouldn't require mistletoe, but you're such an honorable man, I feared you would never take advantage of the situation while I was under your protection."

She thought he would reach for her, but his hands remained at his sides. "Andrea… I'm anything but honorable." His lips twisted in self-deprecation. "There's something I have to tell you."

Chapter Seven

Alarm darted through her. "What?"

"You haven't been under my protection since this afternoon."

Her brows knit together. "I don't understand."

"Your husband has been arrested, but I made the decision to give you the news as a Christmas present tomorrow morning."

Andrea heard the explanation, but it took a second for it to compute. The danger to her and Jack was over! But overriding her relief was a growing excitement that Flynn hadn't wanted to tell her yet.

Was it really because he thought it would make the best Christmas present? Or was there more behind it?

I have to find out.

"Since you changed your mind and have given me my gift now, then let me thank you now."

In a daring move, she took the few steps needed to reach Flynn and cupped his striking face in her hands. Standing on tiptoe, she pressed her lips to the mouth she'd been needing to taste.

When he didn't respond, Andrea wanted to die. "I'm sorry," she whispered, mortified that she'd taken the initiative before realizing she'd misunderstood.

She started to turn away, but in an unexpected move, he pulled her fully into his arms.

"For what?" he half groaned the words into her hair. "I've been waiting for a sign that you wouldn't be frightened to death if I kissed you after only knowing you three days."

Andrea let out a nervous laugh. "I think at this point I'll be frightened to death if you don't."

With slow deliberation his mouth roved over her features until it finally found hers. In taking his time, he aroused her hunger to a feverish pitch. Andrea put her arms around his neck, melting against him to get closer. They kissed with full-blown passion, bypassing the normal steps along the way. Unconscious of time, they swayed back and forth, giving each other mindless pleasure.

The earth tilted as he picked her up and laid her on the couch, then followed her down. His hard-muscled legs tangled with hers, sending exquisite sensations through her body. As they clung to each other, Andrea didn't know when one kiss ended and another one began. All she understood was that she didn't want this rapture to stop.

"Andrea—" His voice sounded husky. "I want you."

"I hear you," she answered from her druggedlike state. "We're the perfect storm, ready to happen. Alone together on Christmas Eve. You're missing your wife, I'm missing the man I thought I'd married."

The latter wasn't true, but she'd said it for fear she'd blurt out that she'd fallen madly in love with Flynn. Nothing could be a bigger turnoff for him than to have to deal with a lovesick woman who wouldn't go away now that the danger was over. Before and after Michelle, he'd been fighting off women. Andrea wasn't naive and knew exactly what she had to do not to fit into that category.

She kissed his eyes and nose, then covered his mouth one more time. "I didn't think I could be this attracted to any man again. It just proves the resiliency of the human spirit when there's the right chemistry."

His body stilled for a moment. "You think that's all this is? Chemistry?"

Andrea rose up on one elbow. "What else could it be? As you said, we only met a few days ago under harrowing circumstances."

He traced her lips with his fingers. "Chemistry's a very rare thing, didn't you know that? Two people who find it are lucky."

His touch was driving her mad with longing. "I agree, but giving in to an urge—no matter how strong—is only a fleeting moment in the eternal perspective." She managed to remove herself and get to her feet. But taking that step away from him was harder than she could believe.

He caught her hand, staring up at her with molten eyes. "Where do you think you're going?"

She smiled. "Away from temptation, and let me tell you something...you're temptation with a capital *T*." Andrea kissed the tips of his fingers and let his hand go. "See you in the morning."

"We haven't watched the rest of the movie. Don't leave me."

Her heart thudded in her chest. "Don't say that again, or I might not," she warned. "While you sleep in, Jack and I are going to cook you a humongous breakfast."

"You don't need to go to that trouble."

"I want to. Since I couldn't get to a store to buy you a present, it will have to do since it's the only way t-to thank you for your hospitality." Her voice faltered at the last. "You know what I think, Captain Patterson? I think you're really a Christmas angel who flew in from the North Pole to rescue Jack and bless our lives. Good night."

THE NEXT MORNING Andrea looked up from the crepe she was eating. "I heard a car in your driveway."

Flynn was already on his feet. "I'll find out who it is." He supposed it could be someone from the department dropping off a fruit basket. They'd given him one last year.

Jack was in the playpen next to them, happily biting on his toys. Flynn moved past him and headed for the front door. When he opened it, he was shocked to see his sisters and their families climbing out of a rental van.

"Uncle Flynn!" Brent and Kevin, seven and nine respectively, flew toward him and hugged him around the waist before running into the house. Cindy, the four-year-old, trailed them.

"Merry Christmas!" the others called out. Both sisters kissed his cheeks.

"Don't be mad at us," Bethany whispered.

Kaye hugged him hard. "We couldn't stand the thought of you being here all alone."

"Hey, Mom—" Kevin called out from the doorway. "You told us Uncle Flynn wouldn't have any decorations, but he's got a tree and mistletoe!"

Suddenly Brent came bounding outside and hurried over to his mother. His whisper was loud enough for everyone to hear. "Uncle Flynn has a girlfriend and a baby! They're in the kitchen eating breakfast!"

"I'm hungry," Cindy told her mother.

His brothers-in-law eyed him with unholy curiosity.

"Why haven't we heard about all this?" Ryan wanted to know.

Rick's eyebrows rose. "What happened to the Lone Ranger?"

Good question. "This isn't what it seems, guys. I'm on a case."

"Sure you are."

Flynn knew exactly what it looked like. Because of his own guilt, he felt a rare rush of heat attack his body. "Come on in the house and I'll introduce you. She's been under my protection for the last three days."

The next few minutes passed in a blur as Flynn introduced everyone to Andrea and explained the situation. His family was riveted.

"Jack was in the car seat hanging upside down?"

"Yup, and screaming his lungs out."

"The poor thing," his sisters moaned aloud.

The children gathered around the playpen to look at Jack and play with him. But he was too surprised by the noise and unfamiliar faces. When he started crying, Flynn could have sworn he looked up at him for help. Unable to resist, he picked up the baby, who burrowed into his neck and stopped crying.

"Whoa, Uncle Flynn," Kevin said. "He really likes you!"

"We're buddies, aren't we?"

Andrea took the baby from him. "The children are hungry and want your attention. I'll change him while you feed everyone. I made enough crepe batter for another couple of go-arounds."

When she came back to the kitchen a few minutes later carrying the baby in his little red suit and hat, everyone went crazy. "He's absolutely adorable!" Bethany cried.

Cindy looked up at her. “Can I hold him?”

“If it’s all right with his mother.”

“Of course,” Andrea commented. “Come on, Cindy. We’ll go in the living room. You can feed him his bottle.”

Flynn observed everything going on and felt a new happiness taking hold of him. “We’ll all go in the other room. Kev and Brent can pass out the Christmas presents.”

“And then can we play video games?”

“Sure.”

They started with the packages his sisters had sent. Gloves, cologne, sunglasses, a couple of new T-shirts. The biggest hit was Flynn’s quilted fold-down mobile for Jack. He could lie on the floor beneath it and play with the dangling toys all he wanted.

Andrea flashed him a private smile after she’d opened her gift. The red cashmere sweater would look stunning on her. He couldn’t wait to see her in it, but she was on the couch, occupied with Cindy at the moment.

“You’re going to make a wonderful mother someday, honey.”

“Thanks. He’s so cute.”

Flynn’s niece was taking perfect care feeding Jack. But he doubted anyone would ever be as remarkable a mother as Andrea. She’d been alone through her horrendous ordeal and had weathered all of it with a rare strength he admired more than she knew.

Between cooking, eating, watching movies and chatting, the hours passed pleasantly into evening. Andrea fed Jack his last bottle and put him down in the bedroom. When she rejoined his family, he felt a burst of adrenaline at seeing her wearing the new long-sleeved red sweater over her jeans.

She was a stunner. Everyone commented on her appearance. He couldn't look anywhere else while she found a seat on one of the upholstered chairs away from him.

"So, tell us your plans, Andrea."

She looked at Kaye. "I've already made arrangements for a rental car." That was news to Flynn. "Tomorrow I'm driving back to Carlsbad. I hope the furnished apartment I recently vacated is still available. If not, I'll find another one. My next plan is to check out several day cares."

The thought of that little guy being away from Andrea all those hours was anathema to him.

"It's the last thing I want for Jack, but I need to work. I'm fortunate that my old boss has told me I can go back to my programming position at the television station."

Andrea had been on the phone with him, too? Flynn groaned inwardly.

Bethany stared at her. "You're very brave."

"If I am, it's because your brother prevented my husband from harassing me ever again. As long as there's no more threat, I feel like I can do anything."

All the contentment Flynn had been feeling had suddenly vanished, propelling him to his feet. "More coffee or pie, anyone?"

"None for me," Rick said. "In fact, we've got to get going. Our plane leaves from the Alpine airport at eight in the morning. By the time we get back to our hotel, it'll be time for bed."

"We don't want to go," the children whined. "We just got here."

"I know, but your Uncle Flynn has to be back on duty tomorrow. Remember, this was just a quickie trip so we could enjoy Christmas Day with him."

"I know." A grumpy Brent walked over to him. "How come you can't take a week off like Dad? Then we could go horseback riding with you."

He hugged his nephew. "We'll do it soon. I promise."

"You always say that."

"This time I mean it." For the first time in two years, Flynn had plans that had nothing to do with work.

Ten minutes later he and Andrea walked everyone out to the van. After more hugs and kisses, his family backed down the drive and drove off. Much as he loved them, he was glad to get Andrea alone again.

"Did I tell you how gorgeous you look in that sweater?"

"Thank you," she whispered. "You've been far too generous. All those things for Jack."

"It was fun."

"Your family is fun, too. Wonderful," she added as they went back in the house. "They love you, Flynn. To have come all this way for one day to make sure you were all right touches my heart."

He put his hands on her shoulders, needing the contact or he'd die a little. "Mine, too. But then you gave it a workout when you told everyone you were leaving in the morning."

She eyed him frankly. "You and I both know I have to go."

"What if I told you I don't want you to leave?"

Her body started to tremble. He could feel it beneath his fingers where the heat from her skin permeated the cashmere. "Don't make this any harder for me. We both feel an attraction, but our meeting was accidental, and now it's over. You don't even know me, and I don't know you. With time and separation, we'll feel these same feelings for other people."

His hands slid to the sides of her neck. "Tell me what this is really about."

She averted her eyes. "I'm not Michelle."

"I'm not Jerry," he countered. "It's apparent we've both moved on and are free to make new lives for ourselves."

"I won't be free until my divorce is final. I have no idea how long that's going to take. My whole situation is so involved and messy, I don't want you to be a part of it."

"I already am a part of it, remember?" He brushed his lips against hers. "Look at me."

"I'd rather not." She jerked away from him, so he had to let go of her. "Your loneliness has caused you to say these things. Jack and I have provided a diversion, but the minute you're back at work, you'll be glad this episode is over."

"I do believe you're afraid."

Her head reared. "Yes. I jumped into a relationship with Jerry way too fast. He was in a hurry to get married, and I was in too big a hurry to have a baby to realize he needed a wife who made money to help support his vice. Who knows how long his girlfriend was giving him money, with or without her consent? If I'd waited a year before marrying him, I would have discovered the dark side of him."

He cocked his head. "So what you mean is, you're afraid of *my* dark side."

"That isn't what I said—" she protested.

"Then let's prove it, shall we? It would be a shame to let this mistletoe go to waste." So saying, he crushed her against him and gave her a long, sensuous kiss that went on and on until she was right there with him. There was no mistaking her response.

When he finally let her go, he linked his thumbs into the pockets of his jeans to keep his hands off her. "I refuse to apologize for that. Go to bed, Andrea. Knowing your husband can't hurt you anymore should help you sleep tonight. Everything will look different in the morning."

Chapter Eight

Tortured by her feelings for Flynn and her need to do the right thing, Andrea didn't sleep all night and did her packing early. Once she'd made the bedroom tidy, she showered and then scoured the bathroom. With that done, she dressed in the red sweater and jeans, and got Jack ready to travel.

When she checked her watch, it was close to eight o'clock, the time someone would come by the house to bring her a rental car. Though she was a physical and emotional wreck, she put on her best face so Flynn would never know what this was costing her.

After a flip of her hairbrush and a dash of lipstick, she carried her suitcase, the diaper bag and the carry-cot into the living room. The house was quiet. There was no sign of Flynn. He'd obviously cleaned up the house and kitchen before going to bed and was probably still asleep. The place looked spotless.

She went back to her bedroom. "Come on, sweetheart." Andrea picked up her baby and wrapped him in the quilt. "We've got a long ride ahead of us." Which reminded her she needed to get the car seat out of the Volvo and put it in the rental car.

But when she went out to the garage, she couldn't get in because it was locked. The only thing she could do was knock on Flynn's bedroom door and ask for the keys. She knocked several times without getting an answer. "Flynn?"

"I'm right behind you."

"Oh—" Andrea wheeled around to face a clean-shaven Flynn dressed in a cream-colored Western shirt and jeans. He was so handsome, she went weak in the knees. "I was trying to find you because—"

"Because you needed me to unlock the car." He finished the sentence for her.

"Yes. The rental-car person will be here any moment now."

"He just left, but I sent him away well-recompensed for his time."

Her pulse raced with conflicting emotions. "I wish you hadn't done that. We went over all this last night."

Flynn kissed Jack's forehead. The baby wanted to go to him, but for once she clutched him to her.

"We didn't even get started," he responded in the Ranger's voice she'd come to recognize. "I thought we'd go out for breakfast where we don't have to do any work and can talk. We'll drive to Alpine."

"Why? I have no reason to go to that shelter now."

His dark brows met in a bar above his eyes. "That's not why I'm taking you there. We'll eat at a great little restaurant first because I think better on a full stomach. All you'll need is the diaper bag for the baby. Shall we go?"

It didn't look as if she had a choice.

But of course she *did.*

Flynn wouldn't force her to do anything she didn't want to do, because he knew he didn't *have* to force her. Hating herself for showing so little backbone, she let him carry Jack to the car and get him settled while she got into the front seat.

A cloudy sky greeted her vision as they headed for the town that had been her destination when she'd left Carlsbad four days ago. So much had gone on since then, she didn't recognize herself.

They drove the short distance in silence. After they'd entered a local restaurant and had been served their food, Flynn captured her gaze. "In all the excitement yesterday, I failed to tell you that the accomplice who was driving the camper was arrested. Everyone has now been accounted for."

"That's a huge relief. I'll never be able to thank you enough for all you've done on my case, and for Jack and me personally. I'd like to pay you for the things you bought."

His serious gray eyes glanced at her over the rim of his coffee cup. "I don't want your money, but there is something you could do for me if you were willing."

She finished the last of her eggs and cinnamon toast. "You mean before I ask you to drive me to the nearest car rental so I can leave for Carlsbad?"

He nodded. "Come with me."

In a few minutes they were driving through Alpine to a civic building. "This is my official place of work, but I don't spend a lot of time here." He put Jack in the carry-cot and they went inside to the second floor. Few people were about. Flynn acknowledged one of the men before he got out his keys and opened the door marked Captain Patterson.

She walked in, taking a look at the generic furnishings, which included a desk, chairs, computer equipment and a file cabinet.

After he put the baby down next to her, he walked

over to the cabinet and pulled a stack of files from the bottom drawer. To her surprise he put them in her lap. She counted at least eight. Andrea stared up at him, not comprehending.

"These represent cold cases. I inherited them when I was transferred here. All except two are unsolved murders. The others are missing-persons cases. There's so much work to deal with in the course of a regular day, I never get enough time to work on them. Though I'm officially back on duty, unless an emergency arises, I'll be working out of my house on these until after the New Year.

"After talking to your attorney, I found out nothing's going to happen in Carlsbad to do with your case or the courts until after the first of the year, so there's no reason for you to hurry back. Therefore I'm offering you a temporary job. I could use another pair of eyes to see what I've missed."

He'd really shocked her this time. Aghast, she cried, "I know nothing about police procedure—"

Flynn sat on a corner of his desk, studying her intently. "You don't need to. You have a college education and five years of working experience behind you. If you were willing, I'd like you to try reading through each case as if you were watching a detective story on TV. You'd have to go through them thoughtfully, taking your time. Something might stand out you have a question about that will lead me in a new direction."

To spend another week with him… She could hardly breathe.

"You're serious about this?" Andrea was incredulous.

"Deadly."

His change of tone sent a shiver down her spine.

"Why me, Flynn?"

He took the folders from her and put them in a briefcase propped next to the cabinet. "Last night you said you didn't know me, and I didn't know you. Working together on the cases I try to solve for a living ought to help us get to know each other on a different level. Wouldn't you agree?"

How could she deny it?

"Sometimes I need to brainstorm, but my colleagues aren't always available. Your being here gives me the fortuitous opportunity to use you and enjoy Jack's company for a little longer. How would you like to be taken advantage of, in the intellectual sense only, and get paid for it?"

"I couldn't take your money."

"Then I rescind my offer." When his mouth lifted at one corner like that, she couldn't say no.

"You mean we'd be like the attorney Perry Mason and his secretary Della Street."

"Exactly. No romance in or out of the office. I swear it."

If Flynn made her that promise, then she knew he'd keep it, even if it killed her.

"They were a weird couple, weren't they?"

He grinned. "No weirder than you and I spending a whole week together without touching each other. It ought to be interesting."

You mean painful.

"Let's hurry home. I'm excited to get started. You'll help us, won't you, Jack?" He picked up the carry-cot handle and opened the door for her.

Andrea knew he was telling the truth. No matter how long he lived, you would never take the Ranger out of him. That was something she'd suspected after first meeting him at the hospital, but now she realized it was the key to his fascinating personality.

Halfway home she ventured a comment. "Tell me about the murder cases."

"Two men were killed within three days of each other. One happened on Chuck's ranch a week before I moved into my house. At that time I was in the middle of a big case and couldn't get to it for months. That's how Chuck and I met. Since then I've done my own work on it in my spare time, but so far to no avail."

"What's the name?"

"Jose Rodriguez was the decedent."

"And the other case?"

"Luis Gonzales. He was a waiter at the Spring Inn in Fort Davis."

She shuddered. "Sounds like the murders were related."

"Definitely."

These two cases were personal and important to him. She'd start with them, even if she couldn't imagine being of any help. Secretly she was flattered by his faith in her. Never would she have thought the day would come when she would be in a position to do anything so foreign to her world. But it didn't matter, because she was determined to try.

Excitement filled her body to know he didn't want her to leave him yet. She'd been trying to keep her distance, but it was impossible. Every second spent with him, she was falling more in love. But she didn't think that was the case with Flynn. Beyond his physical attraction to her, she didn't know how involved he could be emotionally after the tragedy of losing his wife and child.

It frightened her she might not have what it took to

hold him for long once the initial thrill wore off. The only thing to do was make the most of this week with him and fill each moment with memories she could hug to herself.

After a tour of Alpine by car, he drove her up to the McDonald Observatory to take a look around. They ended up away from home all day. Jack had been so good the whole trip, but even he had his limits and was fussing by the time they got back to Fort Davis.

While Flynn insisted on bathing him and putting him to bed with a bottle, Andrea busied herself in the kitchen making a salad and sloppy joes for dinner. She was looking forward to the rest of the evening. With Jack in bed for the night, she could begin the job Flynn had hired her to do.

Chapter Nine

Flynn went back to the kitchen and finished off his fourth sloppy joe. He loved Andrea's food. So far she was terrific at everything, including being a superb mother. There was nothing wrong with her, and that fact troubled him. He eyed her through the open partition. She was lying on her stomach in front of the tree, looking over the stack of files.

It was a good thing there were papers he could go through with her. Otherwise he wouldn't be able to keep his eyes off her features or the lovely mold of her body. Her femininity along with her beauty made it hard to think about anything but loving her the way he longed to do.

When he'd awakened this morning, he didn't know if his plan to keep her here would work. But by some miracle, he'd talked her into helping him. Now he had to keep his promise not to get physical with her, but it was going to be one of the hardest things he'd done.

"Flynn?" she called to him. "After you're through eating, I want you to give me a thumbnail sketch about the Rodriguez case before I go through it."

He wandered into the living room and sank down on the end of the couch near her. "That's about all you're going to get, because the police had so little to go on.

Chuck employs quite a few hands, and he hired Jose a month before he was knifed in the back out on the range. The young guy did a good job for him and his death came as a shock.

"The feds got involved because it turned out they claimed Jose was an illegal alien. Chuck swore the guy showed him a valid green card, but it wasn't found on his body. Everyone who worked for Chuck had an alibi for the time Jose was murdered."

"How did Luis die?"

"An employee found him in a hallway of the hotel facedown with a stab wound to the back."

"Did the same knife do both killings?"

"The coroner says yes, but the weapon has never been found. Again, the employees in the hotel have alibis. The owner swears Luis had a green card, too, but it couldn't be found on his body."

"So their deaths are two years old now."

"And growing colder by the minute."

"Did either of them have families living here?"

"No. They both sent money across the border."

"Were they friends?"

"Maybe, but no one could verify it."

"How did they get around?"

"I presume on foot, or thumbing."

"The poor things. What about girlfriends?"

"I'm sure they had them, but there are no leads in that department."

"Have you checked dentists' and doctors' offices to see if the two victims ever needed medical care? Maybe they'd been in fights before and their girlfriends had taken them to get help."

He blinked. "What made you think of that?"

"Well, when we were at the jail in Marfa, there was

this Hispanic girl with a baby in the waiting room. She asked if I could spare an extra diaper for her. When I gave it to her, she told me her boyfriend had been arrested for getting into a fight. I remember thinking how loyal she was to be there for him at Christmas time. And that made me think about these two men, one of whom might have relied on a girlfriend for help.

"I was thinking you could ask around and find out if either of them had ever needed medical assistance. If they did, then maybe one of the receptionists or staff would remember a girl being with them, especially if you showed them a picture. Maybe a girlfriend might know something but is too scared to come forward." She smiled sheepishly. "I don't know. It was just a far-fetched thought."

He stared hard at her. "You blow my mind, Andrea. I confess I hadn't thought of that angle. It's not at all far-fetched and might actually yield results. I'll get on it tomorrow morning."

"Are you teasing me?"

"Not about this, and you haven't even read through the file yet. Who knows what else that intelligent mind of yours will think of?"

"Flattery will get you everywhere, Captain," she murmured without looking at him and opened the folder. "Jose was very nice-looking. I'll bet there were a lot of girls interested in him. How sad he died so young. You think he was killed for his green card so someone else could impersonate him and use it?"

"Possibly."

"Maybe he stole it from someone else and it was a revenge killing, or he'd witnessed something he shouldn't have seen and was wiped out before he could tell."

"Now you're thinking like a police detective."

She glanced up at him with an impish look in her gorgeous blue eyes. "I watched a lot of *Law and Order* reruns while I was on bed rest."

Something major had to be wrong with this woman's husband not to have thanked God for his wife every day of his life.

"How about we go through the Roper file. That's a recent case. Three months ago a seventeen-year-old female high school student failed to return home after classes were over."

"That makes me sick, but then maybe she wanted to disappear with a boyfriend, or couldn't stand her mother and decided to leave home."

"That's a pretty dark thought."

"Before we were married, I told Jerry I wanted to meet his family. He said it wouldn't be a good idea because he didn't like his adoptive parents and had left home at seventeen. Apparently they favored their natural-born son.

"I don't know if what he told me was true, or whether he was just trying to gain my sympathy at the time. That should have prompted me to investigate. If I had, I probably wouldn't have married him, but—"

"But you were too in love," Flynn commented, having to stifle a groan. "No matter what, your husband is a troubled man."

Not liking the direction of this conversation, he got to his feet. "I think we've done enough brainstorming for tonight. How about watching another movie with me before we go to bed?" It was either that or he'd break the promise he'd made to her and join her on the floor.

"Actually, I think I'll take these and read through them until I fall asleep."

One brow dipped. "Those cases aren't exactly the

kind of material you ought to be delving into right before bed. You might get nightmares."

She got up from the floor. "After living through my own nightmare, I'm not worried. Besides, I want to earn my keep."

You got yourself into this, Patterson, so deal with it!

"I'm impressed. Just so you know, I'll be leaving the house early in the morning to do some Ranger business, and I don't know what time I'll be back. If I'm going to be late, I'll give you a call. Since I'll be taking the truck, I'll leave the Volvo keys on the kitchen counter in case you should want to go out for any reason."

Andrea hugged the files to her chest, as if she was having difficulty containing her emotions. She wasn't the only one.

"Thank you for everything, Flynn. Good night."

CHUCK'S FOREMAN SAW Flynn pull around the side of the ranch house. They chatted for a moment before he told him Chuck was over at the barn. Perfect timing. He levered himself from the truck cab and went in search of his friend.

"Hey, Flynn— What are you doing around here this early? Don't tell me Andrea's gone already?" He was saddling his horse.

"No. She's back at the house."

"Then I can't figure out why you aren't still there with her."

Flynn had one big reason. "It's a long story. I've talked her into staying until after the New Year."

His friend did a double take. "You had to talk her into it?"

"For one thing, she's not divorced yet and doesn't

feel right about being under my roof. For another, she's afraid our feelings won't last."

"I guess you can't blame her for that."

"Nope. I've put her to work helping me with some cold cases. That's why I'm here. She had an idea about Jose's case I want to talk over with you. Have you got a minute?"

"Of course."

"I want to talk to Juan again. He was the one who showed Jose the ropes."

"He's out working the south forty this week. Why don't you saddle up your horse and we'll ride out there together?"

"You can spare the time?"

"For my buddy? Are you kidding?"

"Thanks." Flynn could always count on his friends.

A half hour later Chuck waved to Juan, who saw him and galloped over. "What's up, boss?"

"Captain Patterson wants to ask you a few more questions about Jose." The forty-year-old stockman got a nervous look.

"Relax, Juan," Flynn murmured. "You're under no suspicion over Jose's murder. I'm trying to get more answers. Maybe you can help."

"I don't see how. I told you and the police everything I knew."

"I know you did, but sometimes we don't ask the right questions. I remember you telling me he got into several fights that weren't his fault. Do you know if he ever had to go to a clinic?"

"One time, to get a cut on his cheek stitched up."

"I didn't know that," Chuck interjected.

"That's because he was afraid you'd fire him."

"Not when it wasn't his fault!"

Flynn felt he was getting closer to something here. "Who took him to the clinic?"

He averted his eyes. "I don't remember."

"I think you do, but you're afraid to tell me. Was it his girlfriend?"

"I never told you he had a girlfriend." His response sounded too guilty.

"Who was she? This is important, Juan. I swear this won't get you into any trouble."

"I can't tell you." His head was lowered.

"Why?"

"Because it would put my family in danger."

Suddenly a light went on. "You have a sister, don't you?"

Still no response.

"What happened to her?"

"She got raped."

"Because she'd helped Jose? Did they threaten her that the next time she went near Jose, they'd kill her?"

It was clear Juan wouldn't say any more. "If I promise to get your sister to a safe house today, will you tell me where I can find her?"

"Tell him, Juan," Chuck urged. "You're not in trouble with me if you don't, but Captain Patterson is an honorable man and my good friend. If he says he'll protect her, then he'll do it with his life. You could help him solve two cases that have ripped this county apart. No one's safe as long as that killer's still alive."

A minute passed before he finally said, "She's with a cousin on a farm outside Alpine, the Riveras'."

"I know where it is. What's her name?"

"Maria Luz."

Flynn squeezed the other man's shoulder. "You're a

very courageous man and will be rewarded for this." He looked at Chuck. "Thanks for your help. I've got to go."

AFTER BREAKFAST, Andrea got dressed in jeans and a T-shirt, then put Jack under his mobile near the Christmas tree. When he was settled, she brought in the file folders, excited to get started on an idea that had come to her during the night.

Pulling out her cell phone, she called Flynn's headquarters in Alpine. "Hello, this is Mrs. Sinclair. I'm doing some research for Captain Patterson and need the phone numbers of the other Ranger regions in the state."

The woman on the other end obliged her without question. One by one she phoned the departments. After introducing herself, she asked the same question. "In the last two years, how many unsolved murders of Hispanic males who were known to have green cards do you have listed? I also need to know how they were killed."

In each case, the staff member said it would take some research and they'd get back to her.

Flynn was so thorough, he would have asked that question a long time ago. But that was the point. It had been a long time since he'd had a chance to work on Jose's case. Maybe there'd been new developments and the killer had struck again. Maybe this time he'd used a gun or a blunt instrument. As she was finding out fast, everything was a long shot. She could also admit to herself she found this work utterly addictive.

The hours passed quickly as she took care of Jack and delved more deeply into the other cases. By five in the evening, she'd heard back from the people she'd phoned, but Flynn still hadn't called.

She learned that over the past two years there'd been approximately 2,600 murders committed in the state;

twenty cases were still unsolved. Thirty-one cases involved murdered Hispanics, twenty-eight from gunshot wounds, three from stabbings. Four of the Hispanic cases remained unsolved, two of them coming in Presidio County, a county that hadn't had any other murders in a decade. The other two cases were in Reeves County, and the most recent of the two had happened three weeks ago.

Andrea read over the demographics. Both counties had a large population of whites, while other races, including Hispanics, made up only a small percentage. What if all four murders had been done by the same killer? These could be hate crimes. Then again, they might be revenge killings.

She made another call to get more information on the latest killing. The Hispanic had been found stabbed in a cantaloupe field outside Pecos. Something told her there could be a link to the other murders. She couldn't wait for Flynn to get home so she could talk to him about it.

Since he was out doing Ranger business, she didn't dare phone him unless she had an emergency of some kind. She got dinner ready and put his away in case he was hungry when he did get home. Soon it was time to bathe Jack and get him ready for bed.

If she'd gone back to Carlsbad as she should have done, then she wouldn't be waiting around for him to come home. The thought of him never coming home was so horrible, she couldn't bear it.

Andrea was in agony, torn by what she should do and what she wanted to do, which was stay here for as long as he desired her. But she wasn't divorced yet, and it wouldn't be fair to Jack, who'd bonded with him already. When Flynn grew tired of her, then what?

She stayed up to watch a movie, listening for his

truck in the drive. He didn't come. Something was wrong or he would have phoned her by now. Maybe it wasn't serious, but whatever he was doing made it impossible for him to get in touch with her.

His wife must have gone through a lot of nights lying in bed terrified because he hadn't come home. This was Andrea's first glimpse into what it would be like to be involved with a man in any branch of law enforcement. Every time he walked out the door, you would wonder if he'd return alive.

Flynn could take care of himself. She knew that. But no one was infallible, not even the Texas Ranger she loved beyond caution. "Oh, Flynn—where are you? What's happening?"

At five in the morning she was pacing the floor when the phone rang. She grabbed for her cell. "Flynn?" she cried.

"No, ma'am. This is Deputy Arnold. I'm calling for Captain Patterson. He says to tell you he'll be home soon."

"How soon?"

"I'm afraid I can't say."

She gripped the phone tighter. "Where is he?"

"That's all he authorized me to tell you. He knew you'd be worried."

"At least tell me if he's in danger. Please. I have to know."

"I'm not at liberty to say, ma'am."

Andrea had a strong idea where he was, but knowing Flynn, he'd sworn the officer to secrecy. "Thank you for calling me, Deputy."

"You're welcome."

When they clicked off, she hurried into the bedroom to get Jack dressed to go outside. Once she'd slipped into her parka, she was ready. After putting Jack in the carry cot, she grabbed the diaper bag still containing some formula and hurried out to the kitchen for the car keys.

A minute later she backed out of the garage to the street, then sped for the hospital where she'd been taken on that terrible night. It didn't seem possible that in so short a time, her whole world had turned around and she was madly in love with Flynn. If anything happened to him before she could tell him…

Halfway there she heard a siren and was pulled over. "No-o," she cried aloud before the officer walked up to the door. She put down the window.

"Mind telling me what you're doing driving Captain Patterson's car over the speed limit?"

"Officer, he let me use his car. I know I was speeding, but I've got to get to the hospital this instant!"

He looked inside. "Your baby's in trouble?"

"No. This is about Captain Patterson." She fought tears, but they came anyway. "I know he's in trouble and I have to get to him—"

In the next breath he said, "Follow me."

When they reached the entrance to the E.R., she parked in the first stall she came to and jumped out to put Jack in the carry-cot. The officer helped her with the diaper bag and they both rushed inside. One glance at the wall and she saw the name Patterson among the list of patients admitted. *I knew he was here.*

She approached the nurse at the desk. "I have to see Captain Patterson. What cubicle is he in?"

"He's been put in a room through those doors. You'll have to wait until the doctor comes out."

"I've been waiting all day and night." Her voice trembled. "Please—can't you tell me anything?"

"I'm sorry. You'll have to take a seat in the lounge. What's your name?"

"Andrea Sinclair."

"I remember now. Captain Patterson was the one who got your baby back."

"Yes." At this juncture tears were streaming down her face. Andrea was surprised the other woman didn't say, "Oh yes, you were the hysterical mother." Once again Andrea was on the verge of hysterics. If she didn't know the truth soon…

"I'll let the doctor know you're waiting."

"Thank you."

The officer accompanied her to the lounge with the bag before he excused himself and left.

Chapter Nine

"Captain Patterson?" He opened his eyes. The nurse stood in the entry. "Are you up for a visitor?"

Flynn frowned. "No one knows I'm in here."

"Well, this woman does. She's waited several hours and is so frantic to at least get a look at you, I hoped you wouldn't mind."

"Flynn?"

His heart missed a beat when he saw Andrea in the doorway holding Jack in his carry-cot. "What are you doing here? How did you know? I told Deputy Arnold not to say anything specific."

"Don't get mad at him. He obeyed you to the letter. That's why I guessed something terrible had happened to you. Somehow I knew you were in here. I just knew it. Can I come in?"

"What do *you* think?"

She walked over to the bed and put Jack down. "Where are you hurt?" Her beautiful tear-filled blue eyes roved over him anxiously.

"My lower left leg has a superficial wound from a gunshot, but it's been treated and wrapped. I didn't need surgery, only a pair of crutches. It'll be good as new in a few weeks."

"Thank heaven. Oh, darling—" She lunged for him,

throwing her arms around his neck. Maybe he was dreaming that she was squeezing the life out of him.

"The thought of anything happening to you… I couldn't stand it. I know I shouldn't be saying this to you, but I love you. I'm so in love, I can't hold the words back." She kissed every inch of his face, then covered his mouth with her own.

At the first touch of her mouth, Flynn found himself devouring her until they were both breathless. When she eventually lifted her head for air she said, "I'll stay with you as long as I'm welcome. Now that you've been injured, you need a nurse. I want to be the one who takes care of you. No one else is allowed. I'll be your legs until you're up again. I'll cook and clean, whatever you want."

He pressed another hungry kiss to her lips. "What I want is to leave this place and get you and Jack back home with me. As soon as they bring in my crutches, I'm free to go."

"It's a good thing I brought the Volvo. We can call one of your friends later and ask them to collect your truck for you, wherever it is."

"Deputy Arnold is taking care of that as we speak."

"Darling—I know you've been through a horrific ordeal and you need to rest. We'll talk about everything after we get home later. Right now I'm going to sit here and watch over you while you sleep."

"Only if you get up on the bed and lie with me."

"Flynn—I can't do that."

"I thought you said you'd do whatever I wanted."

"Well, I suppose I could try." She removed her parka and inched her way onto the bed on his right side, taking great care not to hurt him. He pulled her down so she half lay against him.

"Now kiss me again," he whispered, needing her mouth as he needed the sun.

Two hours later a nurse walked in, announcing she had his crutches. A starry-eyed, red-faced Andrea, whose lips were swollen from his kisses, had to make a hasty retreat off the bed. The noise woke Jack, who was disoriented and started fussing.

"Don't go far," Flynn called to her.

"I'll be in the lounge."

THANKFUL FOR HER BABY, she took him out to feed him while the nurse helped Flynn get ready to travel. When he appeared in the wheelchair a few minutes later, she saw they'd wrapped his leg from the knee to his toes and put a sock on him. He held his cowboy boot in one hand, his crutches in the other.

He had a slight pallor, but all in all he looked so wonderful, she thought she might jump out of her skin with happiness.

"I'll get the car." She put Jack back in his carry-cot and they went outside to a sun-filled morning. In a minute she'd brought the Volvo around. While the nurse helped Flynn into the front seat, Andrea went back inside for the diaper bag. When she came out again, the nurse was waiting for her.

"Here's a prescription for pain pills and an instruction sheet for his general care during recovery."

"Thank you so much."

"The doctor will want to see him back here in three days to check his wound. Make an appointment with the outpatient desk and see that he gets plenty of sleep. That will help him heal faster."

"I will."

On their way home she said, "Do you have any idea

what pure joy it gives me to be taking care of you for a change? After I get you home in bed, I'll pick up your medicine and anything else you require."

He reached out and put a hand on her thigh. "There's only one thing I need."

"First you're going to sleep. Doctor's orders."

"Will you sleep next to me?"

"Yes."

"We'll put the playpen right by us."

"Yes."

"Heaven."

Yes, yes and yes.

THREE DAYS LATER, after lots of sleep because of the pain pills, the doctor told him his leg was healing nicely and applied a fresh bandage. By the time Andrea had brought him home from the hospital and had served him a big lunch, he felt like a new man and could handle his crutches without a problem.

Friends and colleagues dropped by throughout the day to see how he was doing. Andrea had called his sisters and they'd gotten on the phone with him several times. Gratifying as it was to be the recipient of so much love, he missed being alone with Andrea. When his boss finally left the house, he told her he'd had enough.

"Will you put Jack up on the bed? I want to play with him before you put him down for the night."

"He'll love that." She spread out the quilt so her little guy could see Flynn, who handed him the baby rattle. He liked it because he could bite the handle.

Andrea sat down on the other side of the bed to watch them interact. Flynn would shake the toy and then Jack would get all excited. His shining blue eyes looked up adoringly at him.

She had the same problem when it came to the gorgeous man lying there. He'd become the center of their world. Little did he know she'd meant it when she'd told Flynn she would stay with him for as long as he wanted her.

In the midst of all the fun, Jack suddenly gave a big yawn. They both laughed uproariously.

"Is he trying to tell me I'm boring him?" Flynn teased.

"Not at all. But after so many visitors popping in and out, he's had a surfeit of attention and is worn out. I'll change him and put him down with his bottle."

Flynn leaned over to kiss him. "After you're through, come back in here. We need to talk. For one thing, Riley has invited us over to his house for a big New Year's Eve bash. I told him I'm all for it, but needed to check with you first."

Her heart turned over. "That sounds fun, provided the doctor says it's all right. You have an appointment that morning."

"Anything you say, Nurse Ratched," he baited her with a deadpan expression.

Laughter bubbled out of her before she carried Jack to her bedroom. Her dear little baby fell asleep drinking his bottle. He'd never done that before. She kissed him and put him in the playpen bed. Then she hurried back to Flynn.

His long, hard body lay there in a new pair of navy sweats. The pant leg hung loose around his bandage, making it comfortable for him while they had guests. She got a thrill out of simply looking at him.

The second he saw her, he patted the bed. With an eagerness that was embarrassing, she stretched out next to him. But when they kissed, he seemed to forget he had a wound that needed to heal. She forced his shoulders back down.

Leaning over him she said, "No, darling. Keep that up and you're going to injure yourself. If you feel this good already, then don't do anything that could prevent your leg from getting better. Right now I want to hear what happened to you when you left the house three days ago. Don't leave anything out."

Flynn let out a sigh and grasped her hand. "I went out to Chuck's ranch to talk to Juan, the hand who'd worked with Jose. Because of your idea, I asked if Jose had a girlfriend. Wonder of wonders, it turns out he'd been seeing Juan's sister."

"You're kidding—"

"No. Never underestimate a woman's intuition. You're brilliant! Juan told me his sister Maria Luz had been raped for being friends with Jose. She went to live with a cousin who works at the Rivera farm in Alpine where they do winter farming. I called for backup and drove out there.

"No one on the premises would tell me where to find her, so I began a search. Juan had shown me a picture of her so I'd know her. I eventually came upon her in the cantaloupe field, but the sun had already gone down and it was getting dark.

"When I got there, she refused to talk to me and told me to go away because there were spies everywhere watching her. I broke her down by telling her I'd talked to Juan and learned about the rape. At that point she admitted to it, but she'd been warned to say nothing about Jose's or Luis's murders to anyone or she'd be killed."

"So the two murders were related. That poor girl. Did she know who did it?"

"Yes. Jose told her who was after him before he was

killed. I told her if she'd come with me, I'd take her to a safe place where no one could get at her, but she was too afraid. While I was trying to convince her to go with me, someone with a rifle took a shot at us and it hit my lower leg."

"It could have been so much worse," she lamented.

He kissed her fingertips. "But it wasn't. I covered her with my body while my backup exchanged fire. The killer was caught and arrested. He's another Hispanic who works for a white guy who deals in drugs and hate crimes against Hispanics. Maria has been taken to a safe place where she can get help."

"I'm so glad for her."

"So am I. And now, thanks to you, I'm several steps closer to getting this ringleader."

"Oh—I forgot! Just a minute. I want to show you something." She rolled off the bed and hurried to the den where she kept her notes. In a minute she was back and handed him the list of murder statistics she'd been working on.

After studying them, he looked at her. "Where did you get all this?"

"Promise you won't be mad at me?"

"As long as you don't leave me, there's no worry about that."

She hoped he meant it. "I called all the Ranger regions and identified myself as one of your research assistants so they'd give me information. It worked like a charm. I want you to take a look at the Hispanic murder statistics from Reeves County that haven't been solved yet."

"I'm staring at them. The last one was only three weeks ago."

"Do you think the same ringleader ordered those executions, too?"

"I don't know, but I'm going to find out in case he could still be hanging around. Because of this information, I've got to get hold of my boss. This can't wait."

Flynn was on the phone for twenty minutes talking Ranger business and strategies. When he finally hung up, she could tell he was dying to leap off the bed and get back on the job. Being on home rest was purgatory for him.

"What?" he asked as she looked at him.

"I'm sorry you can't go after that lunatic yet."

Suddenly the tension left him. "You know me too well already."

"I'm beginning to."

He shot her a worried glance. "Is it a huge turnoff for you?"

"What do you mean?"

She heard his sharp intake of breath. "Not every woman could handle what I do for a living."

"My son might not be alive if you didn't do what you do by sheer instinct. I've decided that loving you is worth every second we can be together, however long that will be. Is that enough of an answer for you?" she asked softly while her heart pounded out of control.

"I only require the answer to one more question. After that I plan to kiss you into oblivion."

"The answer is yes," she said, anticipating what was on his mind because it had been on hers since the beginning. "I'll marry you the second my divorce is final. Do you know of any way to speed up the process?"

His eyes blazed like silver fire. "I'm working on it. Have I told you *you* rescued me the night you came into my life? I was on my way home to finish off the Jack

Daniel's and sleep through another black Christmas, but only got as far as the car accident."

That was a night she wanted to forget. She grinned at him. "I saw that bottle on the shelf."

"Yeah? If you checked today, you'd notice it's still there without a drop being drunk."

"That's good."

"That's because I've found something much better. You have my permission to pour it down the drain, because I'll never need it. You and Jack are all I want. We have a whole new life to plan out. While we're waiting to say 'I do,' come here and let me show you the many ways I love you, Andrea."

* * * * *